LADY KILLER

USA *TODAY* BESTSELLING AUTHOR
N GRAY

VINCI
BOOKS

Also by N Gray

More from N Gray
writing as Natalie Michaels

Steve Campbell Psychological Suspense Thrillers

The Last Girl

The Bone Forest

The White Dahlia

Vinci Books

vinci-books.com

Published by Vinci Books Ltd in 2025

1

A CIP catalogue record for this book is available from the British Library.
Paperback ISBN: 9781036702557

Chapter One

THE MAN WATCHED her through the restaurant window.

She nervously tucked strands of hair behind her ear while ordering a drink with the server.

Her smile captivated him. Affection blossomed in his chest as he hoped that this time she'd be different. She had to be. This time, she'd choose him. Even in their correspondence, she spoke with respect and kindness. She seemed different in her own special way.

She smiled at the server, and he couldn't help but smile at her.

Yes! She was different.

The man pinched the stem between his index finger and thumb; the thorn tearing his skin. He sucked the tiny wound and broke off the thorn, dropping it on the sidewalk.

He inhaled and opened the door.

She glanced his way when he entered the restaurant and her smile widened when her eyes flitted from his face to the single red rose in his hands. Her expression brightened when she looked at his face again.

The last couple of weeks, the man had only given her snippets of his true self; a close-up of his winning smile, his powerful hands, or his eyes, but never his face. He waited for this moment when he presented himself to her as one charismatic package.

It thrilled the man to watch her smile broaden when she realized it was him; he was the man she'd been speaking with, sharing parts of her heart and her dreams of the future.

Yes, this one was different and he would enjoy every moment with her.

The man approached her table, not once taking his eyes off her. His heart had a steady beat, and hands were warm and dry.

"Hi," she said shyly. "After all this time, I'm glad we're finally meeting."

The time he'd taken from first contact until they met was done with precision and reason. He needed her wanting more. And he never rushed into a first date.

"You are more beautiful than your pictures," he said in a low baritone, watching his date blush. He proffered a hand. She reached for him. For a moment, time stood still. She didn't want to let go when he tried to remove his hand.

She swallowed hard as she raked her gaze down his body. Her thin lips curled upwards at the sides.

He reveled in the chase and was only getting started.

The man sat across from her, staring intently as she browsed the menu. His eyes flitted from her face to the menu cover depicting a map of tunnels beneath Cape Town. A tunnel ran below this restaurant and was used by tourists.

"Have you found something you'd like to eat?" he asked,

glancing at the menu he knew well. He always ordered the same meal; medium rare steak with a baked potato.

"I'm thinking of having the pasta," she added, placing the menu on the table.

"Before I forget, this is yours," he said, handing her the long-stemmed red rose.

"It's beautiful." She graciously took the rose from him and smelled the petals. "When I saw you standing there with the rose, I knew it was you."

His smile reached his eyes, no doubt settling his date's nerves, and she visibly relaxed.

"I thought it would give me brownie points." He grinned and winked.

"It did." She giggled elegantly.

"Good," he said, glancing around for the server. "I'm thinking of a bottle of red. It should go well with your pasta."

His date nodded her approval, not taking her eyes off him.

The man gave the server their order. While they waited, they continued their playful banter.

They enjoyed a glass of wine when the server returned with the bottle; which loosened the shy woman's tongue and made her cheeks glow; her telltale sign that perhaps she didn't drink often, but the man knew not to give her too much. He wanted her consent. She had to feel as if she was in control and he needed the chase to be real.

Their food orders arrived and their conversation remained pleasant, keeping the woman comfortable in his company.

Then, once they had eaten dessert and drank their coffee, he tenderly reached for her hand.

"Would you like to get out of here, beautiful?" he asked.

His warm smile put her at ease. "A woman as fine as you deserves the intimate touch of being spoiled by me," he said, adding extra charm, followed by a cocky smile.

She nodded shyly. Her cheeks were still red, but the effect of the wine was long out of her system.

The man grinned, pulled notes from his pocket and placed it on the table when the bill arrived. "That should cover it," he said, holding out his hand which she took without hesitation. He pulled her closer, wrapping an arm around her slender shoulder.

She huddled into him, enjoying his embrace.

In today's world, some women still blindly trusted men. They thought they knew someone because they messaged daily with a man through a dating app or spoke with them over the phone. Then, when they met them in real life, they assumed they could trust the man.

Some women thought that by conversing with a man, they understood them; knew their habits, wants, and needs.

But they didn't.

It was easy for the man to sit behind his desk, his fingers dancing across his keyboard as he laid the deceitful trap and waited for his unsuspecting victim.

And the fun was only beginning.

Chapter Two

I HURRIED out of my bedroom to get to my next job, and Jewel strolled casually to the bathroom to brush her teeth.

"Please hurry," I said, trying not to moan. "We need to go."

"Why?" she groaned, slamming the door in my face. "They're already dead," she yelled on the other side of the closed bathroom door. "It's not like they're going to complain that you missed a spot."

"That's not the point, and you know it."

"Then what's the point?" She mumbled.

"You know why," I yelled.

"Remind me," she said.

I opened my mouth to respond when the sound of her electric toothbrush switching on followed by her humming some tune. I exhaled a frustrated breath and shook my head.

My fourteen-year-old tested my patience daily. If it's not taking her time on purpose, then it's rushing me so she could meet up with friends. Or rolling her eyes when I spooned vegetables onto her plate or refused to buy fizzy cool drinks.

"This is my company, and Detective Boshoff asked for me personally."

The toothbrush was switched off, and the door opened.

"Ugh, isn't he like old?" she said, rolling her eyes. Her eyes were the same color as mine; one green, the other hazel with flecks of green near the pupil.

"He's near retirement age and it's not a date. It's a working relationship." I frowned.

Piet was a friend who helped by referring cleaning jobs to my company. He was a detective for the South African Police Service and near retirement. He always referred my company to families who needed a room cleaned where a family member had died. Some scenes were gruesome, others were just sad.

Unfortunately, unless the families had insurance to pay for my services, the family paid for the cost of the clean-up. They had the option to clean the room themselves. But so far, nobody wanted to. They always called me in the end.

"Fine," Jewel groaned as she exited the bathroom and entered her bedroom to get dressed. "Does that mean I'm going to Dad now already?"

"Yes, hon, I'm sorry. I know it's my weekend, but it's only for a couple of hours. I promise I'll make it up to you."

She peered around the doorjamb, eyebrows raised. "Aaaanything...?" She drawled out slowly, followed by a sly grin.

"I know what you're thinking and no, not anything. I will make up for it though."

She alluded to tickets to a band that was coming to Cape Town shores. I'd already said no to her going. She was only fourteen and the crowd going were young adults. They served alcohol at the venue and people got up to all kinds of mischief. There was no way I'd allow my daughter to attend with much older friends. Just because I did things like that at her age didn't mean she could.

"Ugh, you're no fun." She slammed her bedroom door.

"Thanks, babycakes. I love you, too." I sang as I walked past.

I collected my supplies from the garage and placed them in the back of my Ford Ranger. As I came back into the house, Jewel came out of her bedroom. Her bottom lip stuck out, and she averted her eyes. She slung her backpack over her shoulder and brushed past me.

"Just take me to Dad already," she grumbled, heading towards my car.

"I'll be right out, just getting my gloves."

I wore extra strength suits when going to violent crime scenes, including industrial strength gloves. With this suit, I could work for the CDC, but I'd rather be safe than sorry; Blood-Borne Pathogens could cause diseases should my suit tear and I got injured.

I packed my bag, locked up the house, and climbed into the Ford.

Jewel was all teen-doom-and-gloom; I could almost picture a storm cloud over her head. When something didn't go her way, she moped as she did now.

I exhaled audibly, started the engine, and merged into the traffic. The trip down the main road to Will's shop was quiet for this time of the morning; it was winter, windy, and wet. I enjoyed the winter months; it was cooler and the best time to go wine tasting.

Once we reached Beach Road in Strand, I saw the first signs of life; the surf club came into view. The parking spaces on both sides of the street were occupied by vehicles belonging to surfers. If the weather was good, surfers were normally out on the waves early in the morning before others enjoyed their morning walk.

Today was no different as I passed Will's shop in search of an open parking space. I found a spot and parked the car around the corner from the surf shop.

The surf shop had belonged to Will's father, who died a few years ago. Will renovated the shop with the money he borrowed from me and didn't make enough profit to repay me yet.

We climbed out of the car, and I pressed the fob to lock it. Although I would only be gone a few minutes and the neighborhood was safe enough. Criminals still took chances when an opportunity arose.

I walked with Jewel towards the entrance of the surf shop, even though she was old enough to walk the short distance without me policing her.

Surfboards took up most of the space near the entrance, followed by swimming costumes, wet suits, snorkels, and other knick-knacks tourists loved to buy. There was a small coffee station on the far side where customers could buy takeaway coffee.

"Can I get a hug?" I asked, standing in the doorjamb.

Jewel turned around and snaked her arms around me. I clung to her like it was the end of the world.

"Hey, honey," Will said, entering the shop from one of his back rooms.

I let go of Jewel.

He set the box he carried on the counter beside me. I peered inside to find it filled with cellphone covers.

"Branching out I see." I pulled a pink cover with bedazzled studs out to show Jewel, and she giggled.

"It's winter. Business is slow."

"You've been saying that since you started here," I said, my words clipped.

"Don't start with me, Ophelia," Will said, giving me the stink eye. He brought Jewel into an embrace and kissed the top of her head. "How's my favorite girl doing?"

"I'm fine, Daddy. Mr. Jones is happy my grades have improved and welcomed me back on the Minecraft team."

"What? I didn't know you were off the team." He glared daggers at me, silently criticizing me for not telling him. Will was part of her life, too. He should know what's going on, or ask her how she's doing and not assume that everything was perfect or wait for me to bring it up.

"It was only for the term." Jewel smiled, letting go of her father. "Bye, Mom. Call me when you're done, please." I heard the plea in her tone. She tried to smile, but I saw the disappointment in her expression. It pained me to leave her. If I didn't have this company, I wouldn't be able to afford the things I wanted to give her. At the moment I didn't have anyone to watch over her, and would never leave her home alone. Will was my only backup babysitter.

When Jewel disappeared around the back, Will leaned towards me, his breath reeking of beer. He held out his hand and said, "Can you spare some change?"

"What do you need this time?" I rolled my eyes.

"I want to buy Jewel a pizza or something. Maybe she and I can have fun while you're out doing who knows what—"

"Work, Will, I work hard for the money I give you." I snapped, slapping his outstretched hand away and pulled out my cellphone. "I don't have cash on me, but I'll transfer money into your account. Only enough for pizza—"

"And a bottle of wine for me?" he said, wearing an obnoxious smile.

"Buy your own damn alcohol with your own money."

"Oh, come on," he grumbled. "See, this is why we never stayed together."

"No," — I pointed my index finger into his chest, — "we divorced when I realized you were a leach and would never amount to anything. The only reason I keep you around—" I bit my tongue when Jewel entered the shop, earphones in her ears, but the expression she wore told me she had heard.

I exhaled and counted to ten. I swiped my phone open and tapped on the banking app. When I raised my phone to my face, it automatically entered my account. Sending Will money daily was killing my credit score rating.

I sent enough money for a pizza and glared at Will. His scowl only fueled my anger.

To get to Jewel, I moved around Will, but he stood like a statue, blocking my path. "Get out of my way," I said through gritted teeth, glaring at him. When he didn't move, I pushed him. I reached for Jewel and brought her in for another hug. "Bye, hon, Mama loves you," I said, kissing the top of her head and dragging a strand of her hair through my fingers. "Watch your Dad. It seems he needs the babysitter."

I brushed past Will again, elbowing him in his side, and left my daughter with her deadbeat dad.

Will yelled something as I left, but I ignored the insult. I didn't want to get into another fight with him in front of Jewel. She'd gone through enough these few years and I didn't think it was worth the effort.

Instead, I showed his shop my middle finger and felt instantly better. I climbed into my new vehicle and exhaled a frustrated breath. I had purchased the vehicle recently and Will kept asking about it. He'd moaned I had money to buy a new Ford, but not enough to help him out. What he failed to understand; I needed a car large enough for my gear, and sometimes the locations we were called to were remote. If I purchased a van, it could get stuck on the gravel road if it was wet. Plus, I was paying off the Ford monthly; I didn't pay cash for it upfront.

My cellphone beeped and I pulled it out of my pocket. Lucy, my business partner, sent me a text message saying she would be a few minutes late.

I shook my head and threw my cellphone into the center console. This was another scene I'd have to do alone.

Chapter Three

THE ROAD to the small farm holding in Stellenbosch, near Polkadraai Strawberry Farm and Spier Wine Farm, was scenic. The road on both sides had vineyards and farms surrounded by mountains. I'd driven this road plenty of times before when I indulged in wine tastings. But lately, I'd been so busy with work I hadn't had time to do grocery shopping, never mind indulging in the latest wines.

The tires of my Ford crunched on the gravel as I drove up the secluded driveway. The victim lived on a small farm holding between wine farms. On the property, they had a greenhouse filled with plants to the right.

I parked behind one of the South African Police Service cars and collected my things out of the back.

"Hi, Miss Ophelia," Jacob said, leaning his bicycle against a tree and approached. "Let me help."

"Thanks, Jacob." I handed him the cleaning equipment and bucket. "I didn't know you were coming today."

"Miss Lucy said you might need my help."

"Okay, great," I said with a smile even though it

angered me that Lucy might not make it. "Did you ride your bicycle all the way here?"

"Yes, Miss Ophelia," he smiled. His teeth were the whitest I'd ever seen. His skin was dark and smooth for a man of almost fifty. "My home was nearby." He pointed at an area in the distance known as Blue Downs, where gang-sterism was on the rise. I'd forgotten Jacob lived there. Every day he battled the streets on his bike to get to the taxi rank and then to the crime scene to help clean. And no matter how many times I told him to call me Ophelia, he continued calling me Miss Ophelia.

"Have you gone for your driver's license yet?" I asked as I removed our suits.

"I'm going on Tuesday."

"Good, let me know if you get it and I'll bring my old car to you. And in the meantime, we need to find you another accommodation. What happened to the room we arranged with the estate agent?"

"It was already taken," he said without looking at me.

I set my things down again in the back of my Ford and pulled out my cellphone. I dialed the number of an acquaintance who worked in real estate. When I got hold of her, I asked her to find accommodation for Jacob and that both he and I would view the property together. I told her about his situation, and she browsed the rentals while I waited for her feedback. She gave me details for properties close to my home in Somerset West, and another one in Gordon's Bay.

I sighed as I imagined how hard it was for Jacob when I felt this way. Unfortunately, there were still those who felt they were superior based on the color of their skin, making the lives of others that much harder.

I might not have been born in South Africa, but I was a

South African. I understood the hardships of the majority, but I also hated politics and avoided the subject when brought up. All I wanted, apart from world peace, was for everyone to treat each other with love, kindness, and compassion.

"When we're done here, we're going to see a place near me and one in Gordon's Bay," I said once I made the arrangements with the owners.

He turned around and smiled, his eyes shining like stars. "Thank you, Miss Ophelia, I'd like that."

"My pleasure, Jacob. And I know you feel uncomfortable phoning me, but you must when things don't work out. I can help. I thought you had already moved into the small apartment last week during your leave."

Jacob nodded, turned around and headed towards the house. He was a timid man who never said a bad thing about anyone. And he was a hard worker. He started working for me as my gardener and when I started working as a crime scene cleaner, I offered him a job with a substantial pay increase. He could afford to buy himself a car and rent a three-bedroom apartment, but he preferred to save money so that I could send a portion of it to his family, who still lived in Mozambique. Although Jacob was a South African Citizen, he met his wife when the army sent him to Mozambique. For now, they would stay there until he bought himself a house and then reunite with his wife and children.

Detective Piet Boshoff exited the house, slapped Jacob on the shoulder in greeting, and approached me.

"Do you need a hand?" he asked, taking the biohazard container out of my hands without waiting for my answer.

"Hi Piet, thanks," I closed the back of the Ford and followed him inside. "You were very vague on the phone.

What kind of crime scene is this?" I glanced at my surroundings, noting the grass and flowerbed needed water.

He exhaled and shook his head. I'd never seen him this frazzled before.

"It's nothing I've seen before, O." Piet struggled to say my name with his Afrikaans accent and resorted to just calling me O, reminding me of Oprah. I smiled, but I quickly squashed it when I smelled the stench.

Jacob had already started setting everything up outside the house near the front door. I handed him a suit, and he started climbing into it.

I poked my head through the door, and bile rose, forcing me to swallow hard.

"Ya, it's a bad one." Piet set the biohazard container on the ground near the door. "Her air conditioner was left on a hot temperature for two days before the helper found her body." He exhaled frustratingly. "And to think I wanted to retire this month." He rubbed his eyes, then his cheeks. "If I don't solve this one, it will keep haunting me until I die."

I'd seen my fair share of bloody crime scenes, but whatever had happened to this victim was gruesome. There was blood everywhere and from that glimpse, some parts were still moist.

"Is the case that bad?"

"Ya," Piet said deep in thought. "One of the worst I've seen in all the years I've worked as a detective."

That meant a lot coming from Piet. "Does that mean you're staying on the case until you catch the killer?"

Piet nodded, and his shoulders sagged; his job clearly weighing him down. They had more cases coming in daily than they could solve. As a detective, he had to be involved in most homicide cases or assist others when there was a staff shortage. This case was a recent addition to his workload.

I wanted to change the subject and it was one I didn't like. "Thanks for calling. Who do I send the invoice to?" I hated asking, but before we started cleaning I needed to handle the administration.

"The victim has insurance that will cover it," he said, handing me a piece of paper with the authorization number and contact person.

"Thanks." I pocketed the document and climbed into my suit.

When Jacob and I dressed in our personal protective gear, we entered the house. Piet stood to one side with an officer who was busy packing his items away; he had been dusting for fingerprints, but from the looks of it, there were none for him to collect. The two spoke in hushed tones and I could only imagine what had happened to this poor woman to elicit such a reaction from the police.

"Are you sure you don't need the scene again?" I asked loud enough for them to hear. I needed their confirmation that they were happy for us to clean the evidence.

"Yes, we got enough. The technicians have another case they had to rush off to," Piet said, signing a document and handing it to the officer. "I can't stay." He neared, placing his large hands on his hips, his gut hanging slightly over his belt. Piet rubbed his face with one hand and scratched his mustache, his bald head shining in the sunlight. "I have a gang shooting in Delft, near the airport. They caught the gang members, but they need help to secure the area."

"We'll be fine. Good luck." My words came out muffled through the respirator.

"I have an officer who will stay here until you finish. He needs to take pictures for the insurance company and then he'll lock up. If you need him, his name is Dumi." He thumbed at the officer behind him.

Dumi stood with his hands in his pockets, surveying the area like he was waiting for snipers to jump out of the shadows.

"We'll be fine." I smiled but knew he couldn't see it, so I gave him a thumbs up. "Have a good day."

He didn't reply as he left us standing there with our buckets and cleaning material.

I turned to Jacob and pointed to my left. "You start that side, and I'll start this side."

"Yes, Miss Ophelia." Jacob picked up his equipment and headed for the bloodstains on the floor near the TV cabinet.

The lounge was an open plan area shared with the kitchen. There were two couches, a TV stand and a six-seater dining table. The house had modern furnishings, recently spoiled by the victims' blood, which covered most of the floor area from the floating kitchen island to the other side near the TV.

I shuddered when I saw the darkest pool of blood with strange markings where I assumed the body had been.

We cleaned slowly and carefully. I found nail clippings and brain matter in the corner near the kitchen and something that reminded me of an organ. I scooped it up in a towel and discarded it in the biohazard container.

I was grateful I couldn't smell much with the positive pressure airflow full-face respirator mask I'd bought—they were expensive but worth it. To the person on the street, Jacob and I seemed like large white marshmallows, but our suits protected us from everything.

We used fast-acting granules which got into the tiniest of cracks, absorbing any liquid—or spilt blood—easily and safely. Once that was done, we scrapped the granules with the blood spill and used paper towels to clean the mess. We threw all the paper towels in the biohazard container and continued until the floor was void of red gunk.

Then we cleaned again.

After two hours of scrubbing, wiping, and mopping, I met Jacob at the halfway mark in the living room. Sweat peppered my forehead and clothing clung to my body. The suits made us hot, especially when we worked this hard.

I glanced down at the floor. It needed to dry before we mopped the fourth and final time. While we waited for it to dry, I instructed Jacob to check all the furniture for any blood splatter. He needed to check photo frames, furniture legs, and even cushions. If there was any drop of blood, we had to either clean it or discard the items.

It was our job to ensure the room was spotless. If there was a family living with the victim, they shouldn't be able to tell someone had died here. And if they were selling the house, the new owners shouldn't find any evidence to the fact.

We prided ourselves in doing our best while ensuring our safety.

While Jacob checked the furniture in the living room, I inspected the kitchen. When we had first arrived, at a glance I could tell the murder scene took place in the living space, but I wanted to make sure nothing had spilt over into the kitchen.

The gray tiles had no flecks of red. The kitchen cabinets were still white, with clear glass doors. The counter was spotless, although there was a mug near the kettle with a tea bag inside.

I glanced at the front door and back at the mug and, although I wasn't a detective, I always tried to envision what had happened at a scene. Perhaps she had a visitor, but there was only one mug out. Unless it was an unexpected visit, yet the lock on the door was still intact.

I walked around the corner where the washing machine, dishwasher, and dryer stood under the counter. Inside the sink were two champagne glasses. My brow furrowed. I didn't recall seeing any pictures of the victim with a partner; they were mainly pictures of her family and a dog.

I exited the back door and whistled. No dog ran up to me. With my hands on my hips, I exited out the backdoor and found two empty dog bowls. I traversed down the stairs and headed towards the greenhouse out back.

The neatly cut grass was turning white with various flower beds positioned along the path towards the greenhouse. The owner had taken pride in their garden but the soil looked dry.

The door to the greenhouse was closed. When I yanked it open, a wave of heat smacked into me, stealing my breath. Even with the suit, I felt the inferno.

The plants inside the greenhouse had withered and died. From their condition, Piet's assumption that the owner had been dead for a couple of days before being discovered was true. The windows were closed and there was no ventilation. I had no green thumbs and knew little about plants, but something didn't feel right.

I entered the greenhouse, and a familiar stench caught me off guard, making me wish I had never removed my mask. Heading towards the back of the greenhouse, I found the cause of the stink. I removed my gloves and sent Piet a text.

Chapter Four

I WALKED DOWN THE PATH, passing all the green plants that were slowly dying. I'd been a crime scene cleaner for six years, and out of habit, I always looked out for body fluids or anything that stood out of place.

As I walked to the front of the greenhouse, something sparkled in the darkest corner. I approached, pushed vines to one side and saw a silver necklace with a ruby in the middle of a silver rose. It must've fallen off the victim when she worked here.

I understood I shouldn't tamper with evidence, but this item was so far out of the way, I doubted it belonged to the killer or was the murder weapon. But I had learned a lot from working with Piet and his men to know I shouldn't take anything unless there was proof of its position.

I didn't know how long Piet would take to return and Dumi didn't know what to do when I called him to take a look. He was a junior police officer and wasn't usually involved in crime scene evidence collection. But since there was a shortage of technical staff, I thought I'd help before the necklace disappeared—not that I was pointing fingers at Dumi, but previously some valuables had gone missing and I didn't want this one to grow legs before Piet had it tested for evidence.

I snapped a picture of the necklace with my phone and sent it to Piet. I picked up the necklace with clean gloves and placed it in a ziplock bag I kept in my pocket for times like these; another habit I picked up. I would give it to Piet when he returned.

I was part owner of *O & L Crime Scene Cleaners*. It was my job to think above and beyond my current scope of practice. I had a keen interest in evidence collection and solving investigations.

When I cleaned a crime scene, I tried to solve it in my head. Then when I completed the task, I would ask Piet what he thought. So far, I had been right on all but one case; how was I to know the difference between the blood splatter of a shotgun versus a 22 caliber? I knew now; suicide by a shotgun in the face left brain matter and blood everywhere. Whereas with a 22 caliber, there's only a pool of blood. All of this was very morbid, but it piqued my interest.

After I sent Piet the picture, a message came through from my partner, Lucy. She wasn't joining us today, again; it annoyed me but I understood. The last couple of cleaning jobs, she'd been too ill to help. I hoped she was okay. She understood this job wasn't for the faint of heart when we agreed to become partners. But after six years of working non-stop, I feared it was taking its toll on her.

From discussions with fellow cleaners, I suspected Lucy had had enough and didn't want to do it any longer. This job wasn't something most could do long-term. Sometimes, we worked odd, long hours and had to clean over weekends. It was hard on our bodies and worse on our minds.

I tried not to think about the various blood scenes I'd seen or I'd have nightmares for the rest of my life. Thank heavens I'd never seen a corpse—yet. I could only imagine what Piet and his team went through daily and the countless hours of therapy they went through.

As I exited the greenhouse, a flash of red caught my attention. A red rose had bloomed beneath a roof of leaves near a tree. It amazed me it grew in the plant's shadow.

I approached the lonely Rosa Papa Meilland; the dark, velvety crimson flower had blossomed beautifully. Tempted to pick the flower, I reached for it, then paused. The hairs on the back of my neck and forearms stood up. I rarely had the feeling of being watched, but I did then and spun around. My eyes flitted around the room and outside, but saw no one.

Dark shadows crept along the floor as the clouds covered the sun; bathing the greenhouse in darkness. A shudder ran through me. I shook out my arms, ignoring the feeling, and faced the rose once more. I'd leave the rose alone. It made little sense picking it to die on my kitchen counter, at least here it could continue blooming each year.

I hurried out of the greenhouse and slammed into a wall of meat. Piet stood like a mountain in the doorway as we collided with each other. I fell backwards, landing on my bum with a solid *oomph* sound escaping my lips.

"Where are you dashing off to?" he asked, rubbing his chest. He proffered his hand to pull me to my feet.

"Nowhere, I just needed some air."

"Stay here." He brushed past me. "Now where's the dog?"

I sucked in deep breaths of cool air, wiping sweat off my brow and headed toward the dead animal.

"Here," I said, pointing near the far wall where most of the dying plants were.

"It's sad," Piet said, shaking his head. "I hate finding animals and children." He mumbled more to himself than to me.

I nodded my agreement, struggling to find my voice. I tried to squash the feeling of being watched again and doubted it was Piet. Yet, that overwhelming sense of being gawked at remained.

Then I glanced at the gruesome remains of the dog and shuddered. It was not something I wanted to see again; someone had hacked off half of its head and left its insides beside him.

"I'm going to check if Jacob is done," I said quickly, waved goodbye and hurried outside.

"Thanks, O," Piet yelled. "I'll get the technicians to come back here. Maybe they'll have better luck finding fingerprints here than they did inside the house."

I stopped in the doorjamb and glanced over my shoulder.

"Why didn't they check here before they left?"

"The crime happened inside the house and we didn't think to check here. And they were in a hurry," he said, pinching the bridge of his nose as if he was getting a headache. "You know how it goes. Too many crime scenes, not enough hands."

Piet crouched near the animal's corpse, deep in thought. After a moment, he stood up, giving me his attention.

"It was a good thing they didn't need me at the gang scene," he said tiredly. "I went to my police station and typed up my report for this homicide. I'd just submitted it when you called." He smiled, but it didn't reach his eyes. "I returned to check this out," — he pointed at the animal, — "otherwise it would've had to wait until tonight or the latest tomorrow morning."

"Oh, and here," I said, handing him the necklace.

"Thanks," Piet said, looking over the evidence. "The labs are so far behind schedule. I've already asked them to first look at the evidence we've collected from here. Hopefully, they'll look at this within this week. Where did you find it?"

I pointed at the spot. He thanked me and pocketed the bagged item.

I left Piet to do his job and exited the greenhouse while removing my gloves. A strange sensation ran through me, and I quickly glanced over my shoulder at the field behind the property. Vineyards and an open field surrounded the victim's house with the main road farther down. I squinted at the surrounding wine farms, but there was nothing out of the ordinary that I could tell.

Ignoring the eerie feeling, I found Jacob at the back of the house washing the buckets we used to mop the crime scene. He had already stripped off his suit but kept his mask on while he cleaned. I noted a cut near his lip and thought it was good thinking on his part to keep the wound concealed.

"Is that everything?" I asked as I started unzipping my suit.

"Yes, and there were no other blood drops anywhere."

"Good," I said, nodding. "Thanks, Jacob."

Relieved we cleaned the crime scene without having to strip the furniture, the thought of having to haul furniture away on my Ford today didn't sit well with me. I still wanted to fetch Jewel so we could spend the rest of the day together. The last thing I wanted to do was have furniture destroyed.

Once our equipment was on the back of my vehicle and we were sure the crime scene was spotless and void of any blood or body fluid, only then did Dumi take pictures for the insurance company. He also sent a copy to me.

Using an app developed for my company, I would follow up with the insurance company with copies of the photos and an invoice for payment.

Not wanting to leave without saying goodbye to Piet, I found him walking around the back of the greenhouse inspecting the area.

"We'll be off," I called after him.

Piet glanced up and waved.

"I'm sure I'll see you soon, O," he said, smiling sadly.

Jacob and I headed back to my vehicle, and with his bicycle in the back of my truck, we headed towards the owners renting out their garden cottage.

Chapter Five

THE MAN HAD to return to the woman's home. He'd left nothing behind before and couldn't afford to make mistakes now. He had to retrieve the necklace.

Grumbling, the man slammed his car door closed and ran in a crouched position towards the fence bordering the two properties.

Noises sounded behind him. He glanced over his shoulder at workers heading towards the main building of the wine farm. He crouched lower, ensuring he was out of sight.

Once the farm workers had passed, he turned towards the house. The detective working the case was there and people dressed in blue suits carried her body towards the coroner's vehicle. So far, they were only at the house. He needed to get to the greenhouse. But he couldn't go now. He'd have to wait for them to leave and for nightfall. He couldn't risk getting caught.

The man sat against the fence, listening to his surroundings; birds overhead, crickets behind him, and the wind whistling through the tree branches. The vineyard was quiet, except for movement from the workers walking through and heading towards the main building of the winery.

When he heard tires crunching on the gravel and the sounds of unfamiliar voices behind him, the man stood up and peered over the fence. A woman spoke with Piet and then entered the house wearing a white suit. She wasn't from the forensic team he'd seen earlier. She was someone else. From the equipment they carried, and the signage on her car, they were the crime scene cleaners.

It relieved him to know that no one had entered the greenhouse yet. He fisted his hands, willing everyone to leave soonest.

After some time, the detective drove away, leaving behind one police officer and the cleaning crew.

The man took it as a sign to enter and crept along the fence, coming to an opening. He pulled the wire fence apart on each side and slipped through.

The man stealthily traversed along the other side of the greenhouse to avoid detection. He watched the cleaning crew through the living room windows and imagined the thoughts that ran through their minds at the grisly scene he'd left behind.

The man sat and watched them clean for hours; it was hypnotic and calming for him. He appreciated how their coordinated efforts streamlined in the wake of his disastrous art.

The moment the woman disappeared, and he heard footsteps on the path, the man froze close to an open window of the greenhouse.

She muttered under her breath as she neared and entered the greenhouse.

He couldn't see her clearly with the full-face mask on. And normally, the man cared little for the cleaners as he watched them tirelessly mop up his mess. But the way this woman seemed to draw him in, astounded him.

She was not to his usual liking; she had dark hair, a voluptuous figure, and strange colored eyes. It wasn't only her physical appearance but the way she carried herself with confidence, and how she spoke to others. She was a creature he'd like to know more about.

He watched as she continued mumbling to herself, followed by her reaction at the sight of the dog. Then she did something with her cellphone.

The man twisted his shirt in his fists and scowled at the memory; his date had said she had no dogs when he had said he was highly allergic. But she lied. She lied so he would still see her. He could never trust anyone again once they lied.

The man didn't want to hurt the dog, but the dog got in the way. Then the dog barked; all that barking drove the man insane and he snapped. The last thing he needed was a dog bite or noise alerting neighbors someone was in trouble.

When the woman, still wearing her oversized suit, crouched near the corner he desperately needed to go to. He leaned against the windowsill and it creaked. The sound was barely audible, but the woman had heard and stood up, glancing nervously around.

The man ducked beneath the windowsill and cursed himself for being so stupid. He shouldn't have gotten so close. But there was nothing he could do about it now. He wouldn't worry, she saw nothing.

Carefully, the man stood slowly and peered through the open window once more. The woman had turned again, removed a plastic bag out of her pocket and crouched.

He white-knuckled the windowsill; she was taking what belonged to him. He needed it back. He gritted his teeth until his jaw ached.

A moment later, the detective returned, and the woman removed her mask and gloves. The man watched in awe as she moved; her dark hair that shone black, her flawless skin, and lastly those striking eyes; complete heterochromia.

The man watched the woman hand over *his* necklace to the detective, Piet. There was no way for him to get it back now unless he intercepted Piet, but that would cause many issues for him. He would have to let this necklace go; he knew they wouldn't find any traces of him on it, but still, it was his favorite necklace.

No, the man pondered another idea. He wanted to do something else. The man silently retreated to the hole in the fence and to his vehicle. He would follow the woman from the turnoff.

Chapter Six

JACOB and I viewed the two rental properties; the one nearest my place seemed okay for the price and Jacob liked it. He said anything was better than his current accommodations in the informal settlement.

We arranged for him to move in tomorrow and I paid the deposit as we spoke with the owner. Once payment went through, she handed Jacob his bachelor apartment key. It relieved me to see the biggest smile on his face.

His new home was his for the next year, and it was close to my home; I could fetch him before going to any of our cleaning jobs. And as a bonus, the area was safer.

Jacob was happy to cycle back to his old home from here while I headed in the opposite direction towards Beach Road to fetch Jewel.

I'd only been gone a few hours and her dad would have kept the surf shop open—especially on a Saturday. He had once said his best sales day was Saturday. Whether that was true, I was yet to confirm, especially since he still needed maintenance from me.

As I pulled into the first available parking bay, Jewel raised her head and smiled. She was sitting alone at one of the outside tables Will usually sat at when business was slow. From where I was sitting in the vehicle, I couldn't tell if there were other customers inside the shop.

"Where's your dad?" I asked as I approached my daughter.

"He's inside showing a lady the sarongs." She rolled her eyes. I stifled a groan.

I walked past her and entered the shop, banging the glass door against the counter. Will flew out of the change room, his hair disheveled and pulled up his pants.

"Really, Will. You couldn't have waited until your child left." I grabbed Jewel's bag, stole a slice of cold pizza from the box, and walked out without waiting for his pathetic response. "Come, kiddo," I said, walking my fingers across Jewel's shoulder. "Let's go beat someone up."

"Yay!" Jewel said as she followed me. "Bye, Dad," she yelled, but didn't go inside his store like she usually did for a hug. I suspected she knew what he was doing and didn't want to see any of it.

Good girl. I taught her well.

Thys' self-defense class started at five o'clock every after-noon. His training center reminded me of those old boxing clubs where Rocky trained. But instead of a boxing ring, there were mats covering the floor on one half of the center, while the other half had exercise equipment and weights.

Jewel and I came at least twice a week. After my day cleaning the crime scene and the interaction with Will, I needed to beat the crap out of something or I'd take it out on my ex. The last thing I needed was a restraining order, or worse, he had full custody of our child and I still had to pay him for maintenance.

I gritted my teeth thinking about it.

"Ophelia, and lovely Jewel," Thys said as we entered. "You ladies are just in time," — he said with a wink, — "we're just about to start." He helped one of the older ladies with her boxing gloves.

Jewel and I changed into comfortable clothing and waited on the mat for the lesson to begin.

We warmed up first, and then Thys went through the usual hand and foot coordination and what to do in various circumstances. Whether they attacked us from the back or the front, Thys showed us how to get out of the stronghold.

We had done all these moves before but Jewel and I still practiced like it was the first time learning them; one couldn't be too confident in a fighting situation. Then Thys paired everyone, one male and one female. I watched each pair intently; the male would attack and the female defended herself.

When it was my turn, Thys called me to stand in front of him. Jewel slapped my arm, arching an eyebrow. I knew what she thought. Thys did this every time; leave me for last and paired me with him.

Thys wasn't ugly, or I thought there was a problem with him. But after five years, I still wasn't ready to date anyone. My divorce from Will wasn't pretty; it's only recently that we were cordial with each other.

Thys had already asked me out on a date four times this year, and I kept declining. I wasn't ready; I had a routine, and work kept me so busy I didn't have time to date.

Thys beckoned me closer with the crook of his finger. I rocked on my toes from side to side. He was lightning fast. In two moves, he caught me in his vice-like grip in a bear hug attack.

My instincts kicked in and I bent forward at the waist.

The moment he realized he couldn't pick me up, it gave me the space to turn around in his grip with my elbow heading for his face. I connected with his jaw and spun around the moment he let go to knee him in the groin. He collapsed to the ground, nursing his injury. He could be glad I didn't kick him harder.

I continued bouncing on my toes from side to side until Thys stood up, sweat peppering his forehead.

"Good moves, Ophelia. You're quicker than last time," he said with a sly smirk.

"Thank you," I said and stood still. "I had an excellent teacher." My smile matched his, then faltered when I remembered he would most probably ask me out again. I didn't have the heart to say no.

"Class dismissed," Thys said. Before I walked away, he waved me over. "How are you doing?" he asked, stepping closer.

I called Jewel to stand beside me. "We're good. How are you?" I stepped to the side. When Jewel reached me, I wrapped my arm around her shoulders and moved farther away from him. He opened his mouth to respond, but I cut him off. "We can't stay and chat, unfortunately. We have another appointment," I said, without waiting for him to answer. I motioned for Jewel to head for the changing rooms. "See you next week sometime," I said quickly and made a beeline for the bathrooms.

I felt terrible for avoiding him, but I enjoyed coming to his classes. I didn't want to complicate things by going out on a date with him and it ended in disaster, which would force me to find a different self-defense class. I didn't have an appetite for that kind of drama.

I grabbed our bag from the locker and fastened the lock on the strap with the key dangling from it. We exited the bathroom, and it relieved me we didn't see Thys anywhere.

"You didn't have to be mean to him," Jewel said as we headed for the Ford.

I sighed. I didn't feel like having this conversation with my teenage daughter, so I thought it best to avoid the subject altogether.

"You need to see other men, Mom. Go out on a date. It's been forever since you did anything for yourself." Jewel climbed into the truck and buckled herself in. "You can't keep hiding away from every man who asks you out on a date. And before you say anything," — she raised her hand to shush me, — "I'm old enough to understand Mommy and Daddy love each other differently but can't live together. Now stop using me as an excuse." She grinned.

I beamed at my child; her intuition was spot on. I knew I had to move on. Will had been a terrible choice from the start, but the only reason I went out with him was because someone had said I shouldn't. I rarely listened. But he gave me Jewel, so I would never complain about falling in love with him. It was what he did after the fact that made me reluctant to date other men.

"Let's get Thai for dinner," I said as I started the engine.

"Sure," she mumbled as she pulled out her phone and started going through her messages.

We stopped at our favorite Thai restaurant at the mall in Somerset West. I didn't feel like eating here, so we ordered take-aways and waited at a table near the entrance reserved for patrons who ordered their food to-go.

As we waited, a man entered the restaurant, ordered, then sat at the table across from us. His eyes flitted from Jewel, who was still engrossed with her phone, to me. I smiled at him when he smiled at me. He had perfect teeth, large hazel-colored eyes and neat, short, brown hair that was more salt on the sides. He wore an expensive suit and leather shoes.

"I've heard great things," he said.

"Excuse me?" I said.

"I mean this place. Everyone keeps telling me it's the best Thai I'll ever have without visiting the country." He smiled again. "My name's Eric." He proffered his hand.

"Hi," I said, shaking his hand. "Yes, we love the food here, too." I turned toward Jewel, who was still looking at something on her phone.

When I glanced back at Eric, he stared at me for a heartbeat before being interrupted by the server who brought our order.

"Enjoy," Eric said as I stood up.

"You, too." I motioned for Jewel to get up, who still had her face in her phone. I guided her through the restaurant and out the door.

When I glanced over my shoulder, Eric continued gazing at me. It wasn't one of those unsettling-gawking stares, but a more comfortable I-might-like-you glance.

When I offered a half-smile, he smirked and winked before turning his attention toward the server who had his order.

"So... he was nice," Jewel finally said once we were in the truck and on the road again.

"I thought you were too busy with your nose in your phone?" I said with a smile. "He was nice, but I probably won't see him again."

"He must be a businessman or something. But don't they usually send their secretary to get them food?"

"Maybe."

The silence stretched between us as I turned onto the road, heading home.

"Or he has a quiet night in and doesn't want disturbance." I offered.

"And he only ordered for one," Jewel grinned, her attention remaining on her cellphone screen.

"How do you know? You barely glanced up from that device."

"I might have eyes on the screen, Mom, but I hear everything," she said ominously.

"Remind me not to say anything that will get me into trouble." I laughed, turning right onto our street.

"Before we go home, can we get ice-cream?"

"We have—"

"I finished it last night," she said with a guilty expression.

I shook my head, passed our home, and headed for the corner shop.

"What flavor do you want?"

"Vanilla please," she sang.

"I'll be a minute. Don't open the door once I've locked you inside."

"Uh-huh," she replied absentmindedly.

Once I locked the Ford, I entered our corner grocery store. It was one of those family stores passed down from father to son through the years. They were friendly and knew most of their customers by name. Their prices were a little higher than the usual chains, but their service was the best.

I entered the store and saw him, Eric, the man from the Thai restaurant. He was already standing near the ice creams; either I was a slow driver or he sped to get here before me.

I turned around to leave when he called my name. Now that he'd already seen me, I couldn't continue ignoring him.

"Are you following me?" He teased.

"To be honest, this is the first time I've seen you in this shop." I reached for the five-liter tub of vanilla ice cream my daughter loved.

"I'm new in town," Eric said. "And renting a place on this street." He pointed to one of the recently renovated homes I knew they rented out. He must've arrived this afternoon because there wasn't a sleek black Mercedes outside when we left home this morning.

"I see, that's a delightful house. Do you get lost in there living by yourself?" I teased. The house Eric rented was huge; it was big enough for a family of five.

"I know. My secretary searched for the best place and one closest to the office, and that's what she came up with." His smile reached his warm, hazel-colored eyes. "I hope this isn't too forward," he started, and closed the gap. He touched my shoulder gently, then moved his warm hand down my back. "I'd love someone to show me the sights. I could hire a tour guide, but I'd love it if you would. You know, for the authentic experience." He dropped his hand and stepped backward. "As a friend, I swear. Your daughter is welcome to join us if you prefer."

Usually, when I met new people, especially men, I remained guarded. At the moment, my alarm bells weren't ringing even when Eric touched my shoulder and back. He seemed genuine in his request.

South Africa had a violent history; not only in gender-based murders but crime in general. Therefore, as a female, I had to remain vigilant all the time.

Eric didn't mind having my daughter join us and told me he didn't think this was a romantic event. I hoped he had no alternative motive. If he tried something, I knew Jewel could defend herself and get away. Besides, I could show him the best places to eat or to shop. It couldn't hurt to get out and we could do something on Sunday.

"Okay, sure. How about tomorrow?"

"It's a date... I mean, that's perfect. I don't have any meetings planned for tomorrow." He pulled out his cellphone from his pants pocket. "Can I have your number?"

He called me after I gave him my cell number while I saved his details in mine. We arranged to meet him outside the home he rented tomorrow afternoon. I would drive him around and show him the sights and then we could enjoy a late lunch. Now I had to convince Jewel to join us.

Chapter Seven

I GLANCED at the photo of the happy elderly couple; they were holding hands and staring at each other with so much love in their eyes. They were married for over forty years. I couldn't fathom the commitment each had made to ensure their relationship stayed on track, not forgetting the sacrifices each had to make. The way they stared at each other in all their photos, and not just the one on the bedside table, told me they really were soul mates.

It made me feel something I'd been avoiding for some time; I wanted that kind of deep-rooted love. A love that lasted no matter what. It was comforting to know that it was still possible in today's world; that kind of love was out there, but one needed to look carefully.

Next to the golden photo frame sat a golden urn with a beautiful inscription in italic script font;

'A SILENT THOUGHT, *a secret tear,*
 Keeps his memory ever dear.

Time eases the edge of grief,
Memory turns back every leaf.'

MY CHEST SQUEEZED, and I blinked back tears. I turned away and focused on my job instead; I focused on the rumpled bedsheets and the duvet half on the floor. Body fluids stained the sheets and mattress. Everything had to be discarded. Luckily, we could spare the headboard and base of the bed.

My partner, Lucy, pulled the fitted sheet from the mattress, bagged it, and then stuffed it inside a biohazard container. Her mouth pulled in a tight line and her brows furrowed.

"Is everything okay?" I asked carefully as I cut into the mattress. We couldn't allow anyone to remove the mattress and use it. We had to destroy the parts that were soiled. Hopefully, nobody stole mattresses with enormous holes in the middle.

Lucy exhaled audibly. Her arms fell limply at her sides and her shoulders sagged. Her once bright red hair was now dull and in need of a brush, and her expression fell flat, leaving behind one I'd seen before; from the man we bought our company from. He too had that sad, half-dead expression letting me know he was done with it all. He'd seen and experienced too much and could no longer continue.

The last thing I wanted for my friend was for her to go through hell just so that she could stay in this company.

"If you want out of this," — I gestured at the bed, — "I won't hold you against our contract. Your mental well-being is more important. And besides, we can see a lawyer, draft a new contract and discuss how the money situation will work—"

"Oh, thank god," Lucy said, tears streaming down her face. "The last thing I want is to let you down—"

"I know." I smiled kindly, but she wasn't looking at me. She stared at the soaked mattress, her fingers fidgeting with the container, and her chin trembling.

"I understand, Lucy," I said her name so she could look at me. I wanted her to see my face when I spoke to her, that she could understand that I wasn't upset with her. That these things happened to the best of us.

"I want what's best for you," I said. "We've been friends since forever and the last thing I want is for you to go through pain. We knew this job would be tough on us and the only way to know how it would affect us was to actually work it. And now we know. And it's ok. Just as long as you're still Jewel's aunty, then I'm happy." I grinned mischievously.

Lucy threw her container on the floor and walked around the bed to stand in front of me. "I'm sorry, I really am. It's just I... I can't stand it anymore, you know. All this death... and blood..." Her voice croaked.

I understood where she was coming from. I swallowed hard because I felt the same way sometimes, but I also enjoyed the work. Perhaps there was something wrong with me—I could stomach the job. I needed a break once in a while but I could still get up the next day and clean a crime scene.

"I know I haven't been the best of friends either." She sighed, blinking away more tears. "We've been at this for a few years and haven't taken the proper vacation time. I thought I'd be okay after taking a few days off, but I'm not okay. I can't do this anymore..."

Her mask had been off for a while and she continued wiping tears away with a handful of tissues.

"I can't do it anymore," she continued. "I know you

41

can't afford to buy me out of the company, but you can deduct the money I took in advancements. And you can employ someone to help you and Jacob. And I'll take whatever is left at the end of the month until the company is all yours." She waved a gloved hand to the side. "I don't care. I'm going to stay at home for a few days. Maybe binge-watch a few shows," she said, forcing a grin, and her cheeks reddened. At least she was no longer ashen.

"We can talk about it next week sometime. I'm in no hurry and Jacob can help more often. He's just moving into his new apartment today, but I'm sure he will be available from tomorrow. Go home," — I pulled her in for a hug, — "recover, and relax." I wasn't angry with her, and I knew we would sort it out. The only thing she needed to do was not freak out.

Lucy nodded, patted my shoulder and, without saying another word, left.

I sighed, glancing down at the soiled mattress. I'd have to do this on my own.

Piet had called around five this morning and offered the job to me first. I never said no to any job, but perhaps I should start asking what type of crime needed cleaning before I arrived at any scene.

Although Piet usually only worked homicide cases, they had called him to assess whether he suspected any foul play here. But it was only a widow who had swallowed tablets and had drifted off to sleep.

The job went quickly, even though I was alone. Once my equipment and containers were in the back of my Ford, I rapped my knuckles on the backseat window. Jewel sat up, wiping her face, and offered a lazy smile.

We had enough time for me to go back home and shower.

Chapter Eight

I STOPPED outside the house Eric rented, which was only five houses down from mine. After we exchanged details yesterday, I researched the company he worked for and who he was; the owner of an International telecommunications company.

Eric kicked away from the wall where he was waiting and approached the car; his smile was warm and kind.

Jewel was kind enough to sit in the back seat, giving Eric the front seat.

"Morning," Eric said, buckling his seatbelt.

"Hi," Jewel and I said together.

"Are you ready?" I asked, pulling into traffic. "I was thinking of driving along the R44 towards Rooi-Els, Pringle Bay and Betty's Bay, then back again. The road boasts wonderful sea views."

"Sounds delightful," Eric said. His smile brightened his dark features. "The times I visited Cape Town, I usually stayed near the Waterfront, but with me having meetings around Stellenbosch, I haven't seen this side at all."

"I guess it's a good thing we bumped into each other then?" I said, mildly flirting with my guest. My eyes flitted to Jewel in the mirror and back to the road, but she barely glanced at me.

"Very good thing," Eric said, his demeanor pleasant and comforting; putting me at ease.

The trip through Gordon's Bay towards Betty's Bay was uneventful, but the sea views were breathtaking. The sun cascaded on the sea, making the water look like liquid mercury.

The conversation was light, with music in the background. Recently divorced, Eric had no kids and spent most of his time working. He was staying in Somerset West only until the end of July and then heading back to Johannesburg.

As I drove and Eric spoke, Jewel kept to herself in the backseat, her eyes glued to her cellphone screen. She glanced up at him regularly and frowned whenever he said something corny.

Eric had a pleasant voice, pretty hazel-colored eyes, and full lips. He was charismatic and respectful. His topics of conversation were general, and I noted he revealed nothing personal, apart from him being here for work and being recently single.

I also didn't feel an attraction towards him like I did that first time when our eyes met at the Thai restaurant. We had that instant connection where my heart performed a somersault and my stomach dipped, but not again.

Eric was a friend, and I doubted he'd be anything more. My shoulders relaxed with that realization, and I sat back in my seat and pointed at a sign where we could see some penguins in Betty's Bay.

I parked the truck at Stony Point Penguin Colony Entrance. We climbed out and traversed down the path towards the spot. We saw a handful of penguins and enjoyed the fresh sea air. There were a few families who had the same idea as us and sat on the rocks watching the sea creatures swim. The walk along the wooden path on the rocks was informative with infographics. And the self-tour took about an hour to complete.

As we approached the truck, Eric asked if we could drive to Kleinmond. He'd heard the rocks at Palmiet River were a wonderful sight. I agreed, I'd hiked there previously and the scenery alone was worth it.

We headed back the same way we came, and I slowed the truck as we reached the bend at Palmiet River. Screams sounded when I turned off the car and we sat frozen for a second before laughter erupted.

We climbed out of the truck to investigate the screams and laughter and discovered kids jumping off the bridge and into the deep river below. Others sunbathed on the visible rocks while some ate lunch under shaded trees. It relieved us that nobody was hurt and we returned to the vehicle.

After that quick detour, we headed back, passing Pringle Bay, and as we approached Rooi-Els, Eric suggested we stop for a late lunch; his treat.

I parked at the Drummond Arms Restaurant & Pub. There were only a few cars outside, giving us options for tables to choose from.

"This is a quaint place," Eric said, perusing the menu.

"The food isn't bad either," I said. I'd been here a few times and had no issues. Their pizzas were one of the best in the area.

"Think I'll have the pizza," Eric said.

"Good choice," I said, grinning.

When the server approached, we ordered a pizza each, beers for Eric and me, and a soda for Jewel.

Patrons sat at a table behind us, their chatter becoming louder. The two men took turns telling jokes while the three women laughed. Eric glanced over his shoulder, then when he turned back, his expression changed. I didn't know Eric well enough to discern his expressions, but there was something about the table behind us that made him uncomfortable.

Not wanting to make a deal, I kept quiet. Eric didn't turn around again, and by then our drinks and pizzas arrived.

The patrons continued their banter while we ate. The only noises I heard came from our chewing. When the group paid their bill and headed for the exit, Eric stood up and went to the men's restroom.

"He's odd," Jewel said, wiping her hands on a napkin.

"Yeah, I don't think we should show him any more sights."

Jewel nodded, saying nothing.

Eric returned with the receipt in his hand. "Sorry, I just got a call saying I'm needed at the office. I hope you don't mind the rush?"

"Not at all," I said, standing up. There were four slices of my pizza left on my plate and two on Jewel's plate. The server handed us a box which I filled with our slices. While Eric had finished his pizza.

As we exited, the group of people watched us as we headed for the truck. I felt their gaze like weights on my shoulders, and Eric seemed more on edge.

I started the engine and pulled into traffic. The gawking group headed to their respective vehicles, and that's the last I saw of them.

Eric kept glancing in the visor mirror.

Chapter Nine

"YOU SHOULD DOWNLOAD some of those dating apps," Jewel said, shoving cheese-flavored chips into her mouth. "Who knows?" She shrugged. "There might be someone out there for you."

I cringed at her open-mouthed, loud crunching. "Close your mouth," I moaned, frowning.

Jewel stuck her tongue out at me, grabbed the chip bag out of my hands and ran towards her bedroom, slamming the door behind her.

I shook my head. She was definitely my child; I used to pull the same stunts with my mother. I smiled knowingly, but with sadness. Both of my parents had died in an accident when I was a teenager. Growing up without them was tough, but it strengthened me and I gained knowledge about how to be there for my daughter.

I thought about the dating apps Jewel had mentioned and I had nothing to lose. My trip with Eric was anticlimactic; at first glance, I experienced heart palpitations and sweaty hands, but now... nothing. I suspected he felt it too and that perhaps we were better off as friends... or better yet, acquaintances.

Eric had climbed out of my car so quickly with barely a 'goodbye'. He waved as he dashed into the home he was renting.

At least it wasn't a proper date; he expected nothing afterwards. This way, we parted as friends and with no expectations. I owed him nothing. Therefore, it couldn't hurt to find out what the dating scene looked like these days.

Picking up my cellphone, I downloaded some dating apps but started with the one that was designed with females in mind; I liked the idea that only females could start the conversation. The men were unable to fill the inbox with unsolicited messages. I'd heard a few horror stories from Lucy where she'd received so many dick pics that she could create a collage and sell it on eBay.

I sighed. Lucy had been on these apps for months and went on a few dates, but she had said it was difficult making a mental connection since most of the men on the apps only wanted something casual.

I was a romantic at heart and not looking forward to a culture filled with hookups and meaningless sex. But I knew I had to try something. I couldn't remain single forever; I missed the feel of a man's body against mine.

Once I captured all my details in the first app, I started swiping left and right. There were a few mutual likes. Some likes I'd already said 'no' to, some were older, while most were younger.

I responded to the one guy whose response was whether I was sensual. I asked if he was only interested in hookups. And when he didn't respond, I blocked him.

I sighed, showered, and grabbed something to eat and

by the time I picked up my cellphone again, there were about twenty potential matches.

I browsed through their profiles, and by the time I'd gone through them all my thumb had started cramping from swiping left. Then, after much internal dialogue, I started a conversation with a lawyer who seemed normal; if there was such a thing.

This lawyer liked what he saw and wanted to meet for coffee but would be away this week and he'd message me when he was available. I rolled my eyes. He probably wouldn't get back to me. That was most likely the line he used to keep women interested while he saw someone on the side.

There was one man who sounded promising when compared to the others; his name was Anthony but preferred to be called Tony. He had a boy the same age as Jewel.

Another guy, Steve69, wanted to chat on another messenger app. Apparently, he was traveling, and it was easier for him to message me there.

I knew little about all these different messaging apps, but I created an account and once I found his username, we continued our conversation.

When my cellphone pinged, I went back into the dating app and messaged Tony. When I went back into the messaging app, my previous messages with Steve69 had disappeared. I found that strange, it's as if he didn't want anyone to see the messages. Then a thought crossed my mind and I asked him if he was married. When he didn't respond, I blocked him and deleted that messaging app.

I rubbed my arms, the feeling of scum against my skin leaving me slightly nauseated. If this was the cesspool of dating, I understood why some remained single.

Perhaps deep down I suspected dating during this time of my life wouldn't be that great, but never imagined it to be this bad. No wonder I never bothered before.

I sighed, placing my cellphone on my bedside table. When that familiar ping sounded, I smiled and grabbed the device and saw it was another message from Tony.

Chapter Ten

THE MAN STARED down at his latest prize; she laid unconscious with her right hand near her forehead; her left hand on her stomach and her dress hiked up her thigh, revealing the fact that she wore no underwear.

He scowled, fisting his hands, and paced up and down the path.

This part of the mountain was quiet; he'd driven up the Constantia Nek Jeep Track and walked the path towards Devilliers Dam on Table Mountain. This time of the evening, the only visitors were the wildlife and his thoughts.

He inhaled, pinched the bridge of his nose and exhaled. He concentrated on the stridulating sounds of the insects, the owls, and the wind blowing through the low branches. The sounds of the moving water from the dam calmed him.

He opened his eyes and glanced at his latest; she was pretty in a boring sort of way. She left the gray in her hair and didn't wear makeup. He almost felt bad for taking her. But this was for the greater good. Women like her were disgusting, vile creatures who preyed on good men; men like him, men like his father.

When he first saw his date, she seemed conservative, but like the others, beneath her clothing, she was a deprived individual who partook in carnal pleasures in the worst ways; using her body to get what she wanted. He just knew that about her from their online conversations and since she wore no underwear, he knew she wanted to have sex with him. She was so easy to convince to leave the restaurant with him.

He crouched and cut through the strap of her dress, then lifted the material away from her body. He stabbed through the cloth, slicing through the dress, revealing her flawless skin.

The silver moon provided enough light that he didn't need to use his flashlight, readied himself and started carving his masterpiece into her skin.

Chapter Eleven

I DROPPED Jewel off at school, and on my way to the job, I fetched Jacob.

"How's the new place?" I asked as I joined the morning traffic.

"Much better," Jacob said, his smile stretching his face.

"Good," I said, turning left and onto the highway. "There will be some changes within the company."

Jacob gasped, looking worried.

"Don't worry, it's all good, I promise. But Lucy has decided she'll be leaving us, and I've been in contact with recruitment agencies to help us find a replacement. We can't work every job, or we will leave, too."

Jacob nodded, no doubt thinking about the future, too. There was little we could do except adapt to our new situation. We had little to discuss so we listened to the radio for the rest of the drive.

I followed the GPS voice until we reached the residential home in Gordon's Bay that boasted high walls, a security system to rival the pentagon, and Piet talking to two distraught young adults.

I parked the Ford on the pavement, and Jacob and I started unpacking our equipment. As we entered the property via the broken gate, I couldn't help but frown.

Piet ended his conversation with the two youths and I couldn't help staring; blood caked the front of their shirts and their eyes were visibly red and swollen. A police officer took them to the ambulance parked in front of my vehicle.

We placed our equipment on the ground near the back door and started pulling on our suits.

Piet approached us with purpose. "Morning O, morning Jacob," Piet said, sounding deflated.

"Morning," Jacob and I said together.

"I thought you said it's a suicide?" I asked, straightening my respirator.

"It is."

"Why are they full of blood?" I thumbed at the ambulance.

"They tried to help their mother," Piet said, shaking his head. "But as you know, suicides in bathtubs are messy, especially if found days later."

I groaned inwardly. It was true, blood got everywhere and not just near the body. Sometimes they trampled bloody footprints throughout the house and left handprints on walls. I silently hoped it was a tiled home because ripping up the carpet would take a full day, maybe two.

"Anyway, there's another murder I must get to," he said, rubbing his eyes.

That piqued my interest, and I stopped dressing to give Piet my attention.

"But we won't be needing your services," he said before I asked the question.

"Oh, why not?" I tried not to sound disappointed. I would've liked to see the crime scene, yet disgusted with my behavior; someone had slaughtered a woman, and I wanted to see it. I shook my head in disappointment.

"He left her body on Table Mountain. My team just got there and they need me. It sounds bad." Piet fidgeted with his pen, the sides of his fingers already raw. "I don't know if I can solve this one before I retire."

"You're a brilliant detective. You will catch this guy. Is it the same killer?"

Piet nodded solemnly. "They've named him the Lady Killer," he said after a moment's silence. "He left evidence similar to the last one. Her body was left in the same position as the previous body." He was quiet as he thought. "It's the same everything." There was more to the crimes but Piet couldn't share everything with me. Although it left me curious.

Piet glanced at his watch and opened his mouth to say something when his cellphone made a noise. "I must take this and then head out. We'll talk soon," he said, walking to the other side of the garden to speak privately.

"Let's see what awaits us," I said to Jacob.

We prepared our cleaning equipment and placed them near the door where bloody footprints marked the white marble floors. I narrowed my eyes, seeing bloody handprints near the phone on the wall near the entrance.

Once dressed, we entered the house and as we rounded the corner, there were pools of dried blood everywhere.

"It's like they swam in her body fluids," I said, pointing to the largest spot on the bathroom floor near the bath; clumps of slimy flesh in dried blood and excrement.

"Yes, Miss Ophelia, it's going to take us some time to

clean all this." Jacob left me gawking at the scene to fetch the equipment.

When I felt something brush against my arm, I glanced down at a hand holding cloths and disinfectants. I grabbed the items and nodded my thanks, unable to find my voice.

"I'll start out here," Jacob said, leaving me alone in the bathroom.

My cellphone pinged, but I ignored it; I was working. Whoever it was could wait.

I swallowed hard. It must've been a gruesome sight for the two kids to find their mother in that state. No wonder blood covered their shirts.

I swallowed the lump in my throat and shuddered at the thought. I didn't know how I would react to finding a loved one in such a condition and hoped that I never would.

Today I felt numb and zoned out as I cleaned. I didn't want to think about what she went through to hurt herself that way, or the pain she was in as her life seeped out of her veins and drained away.

Voices outside the bathroom window caught my attention, and I stopped cleaning. Two paramedics were discussing what had happened. That her kids visited her weekly and when they found her this morning, the parts of her body that were underwater were soft and mushy. Ick.

Images of gooey flesh and chunks of meat left me nauseated, but I needed to clean the gunk in the bath.

The voices softened as the paramedics walked away.

Three hours later, the bathroom and floors were clean. We didn't find blood anywhere else, therefore it wasn't necessary to remove furniture or break parts of the house for discarding.

Jacob started scrubbing the walls near the entrance

while I packed the cloths we'd used in the biohazard container for disposal.

I took pictures of the cleaned areas once Jacob finished and sent the invoice to the family's insurance. They were efficient, and I received the payment notification instantly. If only all insurance companies were this quick.

Jacob and I climbed out of our suits and packed up. By the time our equipment was in the truck, it was time to fetch Jewel from school.

When my cellphone pinged again, I finally checked my messages; most were from Tony. We'd shared contact details and were messaging without the dating app. He was taking his son to a sporting event and wanted to meet for coffee.

I hesitated, typing my reply. I wanted to meet him but also not. It had been so long since I dated, I wouldn't know what to say or do.

Chapter Twelve

THE MAN MET her at a popular Italian restaurant in Somerset West. He handed her the rose, and she smiled, her cheeks rosy.

He liked her fiery-red hair and bright green eyes; but even more so with the freckles on her nose and cheeks. He'd seen pictures of her, but she was certainly better looking in real life than in the photograph.

He sat down and their conversation flowed like they were old friends. She made it easy for him to relax and enjoy himself.

He almost couldn't believe the amount of food she ate for such a petite little thing, and he almost felt a sadness come over him when he realized he wouldn't see her again.

When the desserts arrived along with their coffee, he considered postponing his nocturnal activity, involving his blades and her delicate skin.

He pushed the thought out of his head; he had already scheduled a date with the next woman and if he delayed the pretty redhead, it would throw his entire process off balance.

After he paid the bill, he reached for her hand and she enthusiastically grabbed his, making him smile.

"Would you like to go for a drive?" he asked as they exited the restaurant and headed towards his car.

She hesitated, stopping in the middle of the road, and let go of his hand. The man held on and smiled warmly, making her feel comfortable again.

"I want to show you the stars as we drive along the R44 towards Kleinmond."

"Isn't it a bit late?" She asked, glancing nervously at her watch.

"Are you working tomorrow?"

"No," she said, shaking her head slowly and trying to smile, but he sensed her hesitation.

"The moon is full," he said, raising his hand towards the sky. The bright moon winked at them as clouds moved swiftly past. "Now imagine the sea as the moon cascades on the water." His words held a promise of other things. "You aren't working, and I have a late meeting. Come. Live a little. It will be a beautiful experience." He grinned and winked. "I promise to have you home in two hours."

Her shoulders relaxed as she glanced at her watch again. It was only eight o'clock.

"Sure, but what about my car?" she asked, pointing at her blue vehicle.

"Give me your keys. I'll bring your car to your home first thing in the morning," he said with charm. "Besides, no woman should drive alone at this hour."

She did as requested and handed him her car keys.

The man opened the car door for her, ensuring her dress didn't get stuck and closed the door gently once she sat down. He ensured that every action portrayed that of a confident man intent on wooing his date. This way, he would ensure compliance from the lady in question.

The man climbed in behind the driver's seat and started the engine. They drove through Gordon's Bay, heading up the steep incline of the Steenbras Mountain. The road twisted along the side of the mountain with breathtaking views of the dark wide ocean.

He played soothing classical music and smiled the entire ride, stealing glances at her every so often; her mouth parted as her eyes danced across the ocean, reminding him of a girl excited to see the sea for the first time.

"When last did you take a drive along this road?"

"I've been so busy with work that it's been years. But I recall joining my friend for a drink at a pub in Rooi-Els," she said, pointing at the sign illuminated by the vehicle's headlights. "I should drive here during the day. I've forgotten how beautiful it is." She smiled sadly, and the man didn't want to know why. He didn't care.

The rest of the way they drove in silence, save for the low instrument tunes sounding in the background.

Once they reached the spot at Palmiet Rock Pools, he parked on the shoulder of the road and between trees and high bushes, obscuring the car from the road.

They climbed out of the car. He fetched a bag out of the trunk, and they walked the short distance towards the steps on the other side of the bend.

They climbed over the railing where they had created steps to climb down and onto the rocks below. The sounds of moving water drowned out any insect calls or vehicles driving by.

The woman giggled as they climbed down the rocky cliff.

"It feels like I'm rock climbing."

"Not far now," he said, pointing to flat rocks in the water.

"What are we going to do all the way out here?" she asked, stepping onto rocks that stuck out of the water and then onto the largest rock.

"I have a surprise for you," he said, wiggling his eyebrows. "Now stand still and close your eyes."

She smiled excitedly and huddled into herself. It was chilly near the water and she forgot her coat.

The man removed his jacket.

"Keep your eyes closed and listen to the sounds," he whispered near the shell of her ear and watched the little hairs on her neck stand on end.

He wrapped his coat over her shoulders and she exhaled, her shoulders dropping as she warmed.

He placed his bag gently on the rock so as not to make a noise behind her and unzipped it quietly. He listened to her soft breathing, the rushing water, and anyone nearby. Everything was as it should be.

Taking his time, he removed the sharp blade, stood up, stretched his neck, and rolled his shoulders.

Chapter Thirteen

I WATCHED Piet's mouth move, but I no longer heard his words. His lips moved slowly as he continued telling Jacob and me how someone had killed Lucy; my best friend, the person I'd known for years, the person I trusted with Jewel the most, was gone.

It was just yesterday Lucy had told me she was leaving; or was it the day before? I couldn't remember. She had messaged me saying she was feeling better. She had been watching tv and ordered takeout sushi. Her message was upbeat, and I was glad for her. But... I didn't respond. I'd been working and didn't have a spare moment. I didn't give my friend the attention she needed. I can't believe I didn't respond to her message.

I swallowed the painful lump in my throat and blinked back tears. I flinched when someone grabbed my shoulder.

"Are you okay?" Piet asked, letting my shoulder go.

"No, I'm not okay. How could you let this happen?" I bit my lip, wishing I'd never said those words. It wasn't his fault there was an evil man on the prowl. But I had to blame someone for not catching him, even though it was wrong to blame anyone but the killer. "I'm sorry," I whispered. A rogue tear slid down my cheek.

"We're working around the clock," Piet said, sounding defeated. "We've pulled in more resources from other provinces to help. But the workload…" He shook his head. "We'll catch him," he said with confidence. "I won't rest until I have him."

"Thanks, Piet," I said and hugged him.

At first, Piet hesitated. We never hugged. We didn't have that kind of relationship. But when I cried on his shoulder, he held me tightly, like a dad embracing his daughter. We stood like that for a moment and when I was ready; I let go.

I wiped my face with the back of my hand and took the tissue Jacob offered.

"Did she tell you where she was going and who she was with?" Piet asked, sounding like a detective.

I shook my head as I thought about what was happening in her life. "Not lately," I said, chewing on my lip. "I know she's been on dating apps, but she never told me who any of the guys were that she saw on dates." I thought of the men I'd spoken with and a shudder ran through me; the killer could be any of them.

Piet wrote something down on his little notepad.

"Do you think that's where she met him?" I asked, wondering whether dating apps should be avoided.

Piet glanced at me and the answer was in his eyes; yes.

I wiped my eyes dry thinking of all the questions I needed answers to. "Where was she killed?" I asked and thanked Jacob for the cup of tea. My knees buckled, and I sat down without spilling my tea. The well-used soft sofa in my office was old but still comfortable.

This side of my house was a room which was officially

our company office. We didn't need office space since we were constantly on the road, but I needed a place to do administration.

Unfortunately, one of the downsides of using my home as our work address was I still needed to advertise our business on the side of my vehicle. We had the occasional prank phone call but nothing we couldn't handle.

Jacob gave Piet his coffee and then sat beside me with his cup of coffee. The silence stretched as we drank our drinks and Piet was reluctant to answer my question.

"Where was she killed?" I asked again with confidence.

Piet sighed weakly and glanced at me with knowing eyes. "Hikers discovered her body on a rock at Palmiet River."

Ice filled my veins. I was there a couple of days ago.

"We're lucky the water levels remained low," he said, bringing me out of my confused daze. "All the evidence remained."

"You must test everything," I said with determination. "I know you guys are good at your job, but she was my best friend. Check everything on the side of the road to all the paths near the rocks. He must've left something behind—"

Piet raised his hands, and one side of his mouth curved upwards. When he realized he was smiling, his face dropped.

"I like how you're thinking but we're looking at everything," he said solemnly. "My team has collected enough pieces of paper to keep everyone busy for months. I want him more than you do."

"I know. I'm sorry. It's just…" I couldn't finish my sentence and placed the mug on the floor to wipe my nose. Jacob handed me another tissue. "Thanks."

"There is something I need to mention," Piet said,

crouching in front of me. When I didn't respond he continued. "None of this has been released to the newspapers but I want you to be vigilant." I nodded my understanding. "We suspect the killer to be intelligent, charismatic, and with some type of disfigurement or visible marks. I can't give you specifics but just be careful when meeting anyone new."

Piet stood straight with a soft groan as he stretched out his legs. "I want you and Jewel safe."

"Thanks, Piet. I appreciate the warning." I smiled but it didn't reach my eyes.

I exhaled and glanced up at the calendar. We had bookings for the next four days that were quick jobs, but there were always other, more demanding jobs that landed on our desks daily. I couldn't complain, we needed the work. But we needed help. Jacob and I couldn't do it all by ourselves.

"We've received a few applications," I said to Jacob. "Lucy was planning on leaving the company," I said to Piet before he asked the question. He nodded. "We're going to be busy for a while."

"I need to go," Piet said. "There's an apparent murder-suicide they need me to look into." He pursed his lips and pocketed his notebook. "I'll let you know if we need anything else."

"Thanks, Piet," I said, and watched him leave.

My computer pinged, notifying me I had received emails. I picked up my mug and sat behind my desk.

"We have seven applications already," I said, scrolling through the various resumes.

"Do they have this type of cleaning experience?" Jacob asked, standing behind me.

"Some do, take a look." I wheeled out of the way so he could read them himself.

"He seems ok," Jacob said, pointing at one resume.

I read through his experience and smiled. "You may be right. We don't have anything this afternoon, maybe we can go over them all properly and then decide who we want to see."

Jacob and I spent all afternoon going through the applications carefully. I was grateful for the distraction; images of Lucy's cut and bruised body flooded my mind, and it was not pretty. At first, I was upset that Piet didn't explain in detail what had happened to her or show me any pictures of her body, but in hindsight, it relieved me. I would always remember my friend as she was before, although I still imagined how he had murdered her.

Jewel got home from school and whistled throughout the house as she went from the kitchen to her room. I needed to tell her about her aunt even though I didn't want to. I got up from my chair and entered Jewel's room.

Jewel screamed her anger and sadness after I gave her the devastating news. I held her in my arms and we cried together; sharing the painful experience of losing someone we both loved and cared for dearly. Nobody could fill Lucy's shoes.

"Why?" Jewel asked in-between sobs. "She was such a nice person."

"I don't know why," — I kissed the top of Jewel's head, — "people who do these kinds of things don't need a reason. They're just evil. And I don't want you dissecting this, or you'll never sleep again." I stood up to leave, then turned in the doorjamb. "I was thinking of beating up bags later. Are you up for it?"

"More than you'll ever know." Jewel pulled school books out of her bag and paged through the top one. "I just have a few questions to answer, then we can go."

"Jacob and I are going through some applications and may have found one. Hopefully, he can start tomorrow."

"On-the-job training?" She asked, her brows furrowing.

"It's the only way to know whether they can do this type of work. The last thing I need is for someone to puke in a new respirator."

"Ew, that's gross, Mom."

"Let me know when you're done."

———

I SLAMMED my fist into the boxing bag with such force my knuckles cracked and pain shot up my arm. I went down onto my haunches until the pain ebbed away and pushed back the tears.

"Are you okay?" Thys asked, crouching beside me. "I've never seen you so angry before?" He glanced up at Jewel. "Or Jewel."

"We learned someone murdered a family friend last night." I stood straight, wiping sweat off my face with a towel, and stretched out my arms, readying for another go at the bag.

"I'm sorry for your loss," Thys said, standing behind the bag and holding it in place for me. "Lift your arm higher when you hit." He commanded.

I smiled at him, silently thanking him for not asking more questions or asking me out on another date. He was being a friend when I needed him the most.

Thys followed me around his gym, helping me where he could, or just showing support. He wasn't putting me in a position to reject him again, instead; he took the initiative by just being there for me. If he tried to ask me out on a date, I would say no; and I suspected he knew this.

My friend was murdered, and Piet's stern warning was at the back of my mind; the last thing I wanted was to go on a date with anyone. It tempted me to remove the dating apps from my phone; I was angry. And from experience, I knew never to do anything out of anger; except hit a boxing bag.

As much as I wanted to get out in the world and look for this wicked man myself, I needed to have confidence in Piet and his team that they would find Lucy's killer. We all needed them to find him.

Chapter Fourteen

THE CLEANING JOB at the nursing home was quick and painless. We mainly had to mop the floors, walls, and windows. It was a high-end nursing home and wealthy people paid top rands to send their family members there.

The cleaners who worked daily did a good enough job, but when someone wanted the best for their parent, they expected the room to be spotless. They also wanted us to use the fogger to ensure we left no residue behind.

We had just finished cleaning the room and were about to leave when Piet called us to clean the murder-suicide scene he had tended to yesterday.

I groaned inwardly as I packed my stuff into the back of the Ford.

Jacob placed the last container into the back while our newest employee, Thomas, packed his suit into his trunk. So far, Thomas delivered as promised; he knew which cleaning products to use when and was efficient.

Thomas had worked for one of my competitors and didn't like their business practices; they withheld his salary while investigating him for being intoxicated while at work. He had said he had called in sick, but then they said if he didn't come to work, he'd receive less money at the end of the month. When he arrived at work, they accused him of using drugs. He was using prescription medication for his body aches.

"I'll see you there," I said to Thomas as I climbed into my Ford.

He waved in understanding and waited for me to pull away, then followed us all the way to the house in Strand.

"Are you sure you want to continue, Miss Ophelia?" Jacob asked carefully. His one hand held the door handle, waiting for me to take the key out of the ignition.

I'd been staring at nothing while the car idled after I'd parked. We were at the next cleaning job and I struggled to get out of the car. I swallowed hard and wiped the sweat off my forehead.

"Yeah, I'll be fine." I lied. "Piet said it should be quick."

"It's a murder-suicide, Miss Ophelia," Jacob said my name softly like he was waiting for me to burst into tears.

I glanced back at him and smiled. "Thanks, Jacob, but I'll be ok," I said, inhaling and exhaling slowly. I switched off the engine and climbed out of the truck.

Jacob carried the containers to the front door while Thomas approached with his suit and respirator in hand.

"Can I help with anything?"

"Yes, carry those biohazard containers to where Jacob is."

Thomas did as instructed and pulled on his suit when Jacob did.

"Are you ready?" I asked Thomas when I stood beside him and dressed in my suit, boots, gloves, and respirator.

"Yes," he said, grinning. I noted a tooth missing on the

left-hand side of his mouth. And his left ear was smaller than his right.

As Thomas pulled up his suit, I saw he had long fingers and short, dirty fingernails. He dressed in his suit with confidence and left me feeling better about hiring him. Although I had to speak to him about cleanliness, especially since we're client-facing and we needed to ensure we didn't transfer dirt from our bodies onto their surfaces.

Piet exited the house with a smile on his face. I smiled at him.

"Morning Piet, how does it look inside?"

Piet's face dropped, but he recovered with half a smile. "It's not a murder-suicide as we initially thought," — he sipped on his coffee and stood farther away from us, — "it's our first fentanyl case. We have two victims," — he thumbed at the house behind him, — "and it is messy. But luckily it's not a lot. We do need you to clean every single room inside. The family insists."

Piet searched his body for something, then pulled a piece of paper out of his pants pocket.

"Here's the insurance authorization," — he handed me the paper, — "my guys are done and the bodies are gone. Do you know about fentanyl?"

"We haven't cleaned a scene yet, but Jacob and I finished a course on the various drugs and how to clean it—"

"Good. We think there was a party the night before and many were using drugs. Then, when these two overdosed, some scattered like insects. The owner called us to kick the rest out, then after we switched off the loud music, we discovered the two bodies."

"Have you heard anything yet about Lucy?" I asked

carefully. I knew it hadn't been long enough for Piet to receive any results from the labs, but I had to ask.

"Nothing new," he said quietly, averting his eyes. "I'll tell you the moment I know anything new." He smiled sincerely. "I have to go. Call me if you need anything."

"Thanks, Piet," I said and entered the home.

Thomas and Jacob followed me with their cleaning materials. The stench of cigarette smoke filled the kitchen and lounge area. There were bottles and rubbish strewn everywhere.

A police officer exited the passage and pointed. "We found the bodies in that bedroom, and we suspect every room was used to take drugs, but this room needs a thorough cleaning."

"Thanks," I said and headed down the passage. "This room?" I asked, pointing at the first bedroom.

The officer nodded. "We found blood in the other rooms, too, possibly nose bleeds, but not as bad as that one."

"Okay. Jacob, we'll need everything."

When Jacob and Thomas joined me in the first bedroom, they gasped at the gruesome sight.

"Thomas, join me in this room. Jacob, take the lounge and kitchen—"

"Are you sure, Miss Ophelia?" Jacob asked with concern in his tone.

"Yes," I said, lying, again. I swallowed hard.

"Miss Ophelia," Jacob started. "Let me teach Thomas how to clean this and you start in the lounge."

Jacob was right. I glanced at the bodily fluids on the floor; the vomit, blood, and urine stains. Two people had died here. We needed to cut up the carpet and ensure the fluid didn't contaminate the hardwood floor beneath. Then we had to clean all the non-porous materials or destroy them.

A small amount of fentanyl could harm a human, and if someone ingested two milligrams, they could die. The possibility of them using fentanyl in each room was great. Therefore, we had to treat each room like a fentanyl contamination scene. We would clean each room twice and come back tomorrow to clean again and use the fogger to reach the areas we couldn't. This was a massive job, and it relieved me we had Thomas to help us.

Bile rose in my mouth, and I swallowed hard, nodding as I thought about the scenes. Without thinking, I left the men in the bedroom, hurried down the corridor and yanked off my respirator. I puked in the basin in the bathroom until there was nothing left to vomit. I wiped my mouth with toilet paper and shuddered. There was a stench coming from the toilet and I flushed; it seemed someone else couldn't keep their breakfast down either.

———

BY LATE AFTERNOON, I ordered everyone to stop working. We'd been working nonstop for six hours, cleaning as much of the mess as we could, but we needed to come back tomorrow morning and finish. And I had to move my other job to the following day.

I sent the insurance company proof of our progress, along with a quote, which they accepted. It was good money, but hard work.

"Thomas," I said, waiting for him to look at me. "You did a great job today."

"Thanks," he beamed, brushing oily hair out of his eyes.

"If you're still interested in the job, I'd like to employ you permanently."

"Thank you," Thomas said, exhaling. He seemed relieved. "What are the benefits?"

"We work together and earn an equal salary. This way, nobody feels cheated. What's left goes back into the company to buy all the materials we need to do the job. You can ask Jacob, I'm fair when it comes to days off or needing personal time. We're adults here and we do everything within reason. Unfortunately, your salary must cover your own medical aid and pension, but I'll handle the tax."

Thomas' smile reached his glistening eyes when I told him the amount he'd earn monthly, and if at the end of the year and the company had made enough, everybody received a nice Christmas bonus.

"Jewel is with her dad and I'm starving," I said as I packed a container into the back of the Ford. "I think we deserve pizzas and beers after the day we've had."

"I could eat," Thomas said.

"Good," I said, climbing into the car. "Let's go eat."

Chapter Fifteen

WE ORDERED our food and drinks and laughed at Jacob's jokes. He was a natural storyteller for an introvert. When everything settled down and our food arrived, we ate in silence.

"So, Thomas, what do you do in your spare time?" I asked while wiping my mouth clean.

"I stuff animals."

I stared open-mouthed.

"What I mean is I'm a taxidermist. I work with my uncle. It's not a very lucrative business, but I help where I can."

I was both mortified and intrigued. "What... how... which animals?" I asked, trying to find the right words.

"It's mostly hunting trophies; fish, buck and zebra heads. That kind of thing."

I envisioned the Bates Motel and Norman stuffing his white poodle.

"I don't know where to begin asking questions. I've met no one who did this."

"We aren't as sinister as Norman Bates, but it is interesting. I help over weekends, but I still need a full-time job. I have bills to pay."

"Do you have any children? A wife?"

Thomas grinned, and his eyes lit up with pride. "Ex-wife and a daughter who I love very much but I don't get to see her often. Her mom moved back to Joburg and I only get to see Ella over holidays."

He glanced down at his hands and the atmosphere changed. I felt bad for him and didn't know what else to say, so I changed the subject.

"How's your wife and kids, Jacob?"

"They're good, Miss Ophelia. The little one started grade R and the oldest finishes grade 12 this year. The middle one isn't doing so well and needs to see a doctor here in South Africa. So they'll be coming here in December."

"I'm sorry to hear. And your new accommodations? Is everything okay?"

"Yes, Miss Ophelia; very nice old lady with her two birds. She's very kind and prepares dinner for me."

"I'm glad." I smiled and felt good. Jacob had struggled so much in the beginning and when he knocked on my window asking for work, he became my gardener and then my partner in the cleaning business.

When we finished our coffee and dessert, I texted Jewel. When she didn't answer, something didn't sit right with me. With everything that was going on, the last thing I needed was something happening to my daughter.

I said goodnight to the men and could go straight home; Thomas would give Jacob a ride home since they stayed closer to each other; just another reason to hire Thomas—he could help with transport when I couldn't.

When Jewel didn't answer a second time, nervousness flooded my system, and I had to ensure she was okay. But before I panicked, I phoned Will, who didn't answer my call either.

I arrived at Will's place in record time. His small two-bedroom townhouse had two lights shining brightly inside. I rang the doorbell and knocked until my knuckles hurt.

"Hey, Mom," Jewel said behind me. "What are you doing here?"

"I've been trying to get hold of you. Why didn't you answer your phone? I thought you were hurt or something. And where's your dad?"

"Sorry, I went to the shop quickly to get something to eat and forgot my phone. And Dad is out."

"He left you alone?" As the words flew out of my mouth, Will parked behind my Ford. A woman climbed out of his Toyota Tazz and wrapped her arm around his waist. Both stopped whispering when they saw me and stared wide-eyed.

"Hey, Ophelia, why are you here?" Will said. I caught the nervousness in his tone. He kept glancing at the woman in his arms and then at me.

I stomped up to Will and slapped him in the face. "How dare you leave our child alone, and make her walk to the corner shop to buy herself food. What the hell is wrong with you."

"Take it easy. We were gone five minutes."

"Liar, I've been trying to get hold of you two for forty minutes."

Will's eyes flitted from Jewel then to mine. "Okay, you've made your point. It won't happen again."

Movement caught my eye, and I glanced down at Will's

date; at her recently manicured nails, and she wore a diamond wedding ring.

"I can explain—" Will raised both hands.

"Is this where the maintenance money I pay monthly is going?" I glanced at Jewel. "How long has he been seeing her?"

"She moved in about six months ago," Jewel mumbled and stepped backwards.

"Why didn't you tell me?"

Jewel opened her mouth but closed it again, the lines between her brows deepening.

"Don't bring Jewel into our fight," Will said, stepping closer. "Go inside," — he said to his wife, — "I wanted to tell you, but it's never a good time with you. Sometimes you aren't exactly approachable. And the money you pay for maintenance goes to Jewel." He pointed at Jewel. "Go inside, baby. This is between your mother and me."

Anger flooded my veins, and I wanted to rip his heart out. "How can I be sure about that?" I said through gritted teeth when Jewel was out of earshot.

"You can ask her and look at my bank statement. I promise you, what I do for Evelyn is the money I make at the shop—"

"You owe me money, Will," I said his name sarcastically.

"I know. I owe you a lot. But I don't make enough to pay you back just yet. Things are still difficult here and I make enough to cover my bills and for us to eat." His shoulders dropped, and he exhaled. He rubbed his face, and I noticed he had more wrinkles.

I'd never heard Will sound so sincere before. He was telling the truth. I exhaled an annoyed breath and calmed down. I couldn't even remember why I was angry; over him not telling me he got married or that he had moved on so easily. We had separated a long time ago and I needed to move on, too. No, I was upset because he left Jewel alone to walk in the streets at night.

"Next time please answer your phone and don't leave Jewel alone ever again—"

"She's old enough. She's a big girl. You need to trust her."

"I trust her. It's the creeps out there I don't trust," I said, waving my hand around. "Women are murdered around Cape Town. Anything can happen."

"Okay," he said, raising both hands in a submissive gesture. "I hear you and I don't want to fight anymore."

"If she's your wife, who were you with in the change room?" I asked, not bothering who heard me.

"It was Evelyn." He grinned naughtily.

———

I POURED myself a generous glass of Merlot and sat on my couch with the television on some paranormal program.

A strange sensation came over me and I glanced over my shoulder but there was nothing; only the vacant kitchen with the window blinds slightly open.

The quiet house filled me with dread, and I shivered. I'd never felt this lonely before without Jewel. Placing the glass on the table, I stood up and checked the bedrooms, and then the kitchen. I opened the kitchen blinds but couldn't see out into the yard. I switched on the lights and opened the kitchen door.

I stood in the doorjamb until my eyes adjusted to the darkness beyond the light and listened. The stridulating crickets greeted me on my left. And my neighbor's backyard was dark; they were probably out of town and forgot to leave their back lights on like they usually did.

My eyes danced across the back fencing and then I focused on my neighbor's kitchen door; it differed from what I remembered; it was black. But I remembered their door being cream.

I flinched when something flew past my shoulder. It was just a moth nearing the bright globe. When I turned to look at the neighbor's kitchen door again, the cream door was visible once more.

I jumped back inside the house and slammed my door closed, bolting it. My heart thundered in my ears as I steadied my breathing. I switched off all my lights and went to the kitchen blinds, peering through enough so that I could see my neighbor's door again. Nothing. Whoever had been standing there was gone.

Whoever had been standing there was looking directly at my house; directly at me.

Chapter Sixteen

THE MAN OPENED the side gate and slipped through undetected; nobody was home and none of the neighbors were in sight.

He stood on the back porch and watched Ophelia walk from her bedroom to the kitchen, and then to the lounge, where she sat on a couch.

She sipped her wine, then stood up, came to the kitchen window, and opened the back door. She stared at the man but without truly seeing.

When the man stepped into the shadows, she knew. Ophelia knew someone had been watching her, and the man felt proud. He felt seen yet undiscovered. And he knew Ophelia would be glad to know more about him.

He'd been chatting with her online, but she had been quiet since he killed her friend Lucy.

The man smiled at the moon. When he heard the back-door slam shut, he disappeared as he blended with the darkness and headed back to his car.

Chapter Seventeen

SEEING the shadow move from my neighbor's door left me shaken and nervous. I wanted to message Piet but then thought it was a silly idea. Whoever was there had most likely left. If I called Piet now, he would come all the way here for nothing. I doubted the perpetrator left any evidence.

I chewed my bottom lip as I paced in the passage, thinking about what I thought I saw. Whoever was out there was looking at my house, was staring at me. They knew who I was or my eyes were just playing tricks on me; perhaps I needed to have them tested.

I flinched when my cellphone beeped; it was only a message. I needed to get a grip. I took self-defense classes and could defend myself. Last year they installed an excellent security system in my home and nobody could enter without a key and passcode. I was safe.

I shook out my hands, entered the lounge again and sat down. I picked up my phone to see who the message was from; it was Tony. I smiled. My smile fell flat. The police suspect the killer had contacted Lucy through dating apps.

I glanced down at my phone. What if Tony was the killer? No, I shook my head. I would know, I would get that sixth sense tingling down my spine if Tony was a killer. Wouldn't I?

What if Thomas was the killer? He was new to the company, and he knew a lot about cleaning materials and how to destroy items; possibly evidence. No, I hired him. We were the ones who needed help. But I needed help because Lucy had left, and then he murdered her.

I gasped. The killer could be Eric. We had shown him the sights at Palmiet River; where hikers had discovered Lucy's body. But I hadn't seen Eric since Sunday although he had sent messages now and then asking how I was. We were only friends; we liked each other but only in a platonic sense; there was no romance there.

Another message came through; *"Are you okay? You've been quiet."* Tony's words were comforting and I appreciated his message.

"I'm fine. I had a rough day. How are you?"

"Im great, thanks. My son won an award at school and I just signed on a new client." Tony worked for himself as a financial consultant. His company comprised his father, an administrator, and himself. From the way he'd spoken he made good money, but gaining more clients was best in the long run.

"Do you want to talk about it? No hidden agenda. I'm just worried about you."

"I'll be fine, just a bit spooked." I smiled. We still needed to meet. His profile picture revealed his face clearly and it included his son. *"Maybe we can meet for coffee tomorrow?"*

"(-: I'd love that. You tell me where you'd like to meet and when."

Butterflies floated around in my stomach which was quickly squashed by everything that had happened the last couple of days. Although I knew what Tony looked like, I didn't know him all that well and I needed to be vigilant.

Chapter Eighteen

WE ONLY FINISHED the fentanyl clean after 5pm. It was impossible for me to meet with Tony on time so I messaged him to cancel. In some strange way, it relieved me that I didn't have to go, but I also felt bad. Unfortunately, I was busy at my job and I was on my way to fetch Jewel from her dad.

I parked the car, and we entered Thys' gym for a self-defense class. After everyone had their turn, Thys called me up; I'd be fighting him again. I furrowed my brow and took position.

Thys smiled sweetly. My frown deepened. He chuckled. I stalked around him, waiting for his attack. But Thys just stood there staring at me. I shrugged. Thys lunged at me. I blocked his attack, hit his jaw, spun around and elbowed him in the diaphragm. He doubled over, nursing a bloody mouth.

"Oh crap," I said. "Are you okay?" I didn't think I'd hit him so hard, but I managed to split his lip and he spat out blood.

"That's a good hit, Ophelia, but remember, we're practicing." He sounded more wounded than he looked.

Guilt ripped through me, and I rubbed his shoulders. "Oh my gods. I'm so sorry, I didn't mean to hit you so hard. A lot has been going on."

"Aah," Thys said, standing straight. "It's ok. I've never hurt this much before during a session, but there's a first for everything, I suppose." He smiled, but it didn't reach his eyes.

"Let me take you for a coffee as a peace token."

"Like a date?" He grinned.

"No, just as friends." My eyes flitted to Jewel, who approached.

Jewel patted his shoulder. "Mom's vicious. I'd be careful around her if I were you."

"I've noticed. Aah," he said, licking his still-bleeding lip.

I felt awful for hitting him so hard. "So what do you say? A quick coffee?"

"Sure," he said, smiling. "Why not."

———

ONCE JEWEL and I showered and dressed, we waited for Thys to close his gym. It was early evening and most of the shops and restaurants were still open. We walked to a coffee shop around the corner and found a table near the back.

"Sorry about earlier," I said, breaking the silence. "Do you remember my friend Lucy? She joined us at the gym a few times."

Thys nodded. "Uh-huh," he mumbled while perusing the menu. "I remember her."

"She's the family friend who was murdered recently."

Thys glanced up, his mouth gaping open. "Do you know what happened?"

I gave him a short version of what Piet had told me. I'd already said most of it to Jewel beforehand, so there wasn't something new that would shock her.

Jewel wiped her nose with a paper napkin and continued reading her menu like her life depended on it. I couldn't blame her. My chest tightened each time I thought about Lucy and how they killed her.

"I'm so sorry for your loss. You two were best friends?" Thys asked.

"Yes, we'd known each other for years and we had a lot in common. So naturally, we gravitated towards each other."

We ordered our drinks and a light snack. The coffee shop had little on offer besides muffins, croissants, or toasted sandwiches.

When the server left, I told Thys how Lucy and I were both orphaned in our early twenties and we married young, too. The more I spoke about Lucy and our fun times together, the better I felt. I shed a tear or five, but a weight lifted off my shoulders. The heaviness in my chest seemed to lighten as I relived happier times with my best friend.

We enjoyed our light snack and coffee while the conversation flowed easily.

"Tell us more about yourself, Thys. We know you've had the gym for years."

Thys wiped his hands and mouth with a napkin. It was then I noticed the scar across his chin. He always had stubble and it was hard to miss unless close enough to see the white raised scar. It wasn't a large scar and I doubted he was self-conscious about it unless he was and that was the reason why he didn't shave often.

He coughed into his hand to clear his throat. "I moved to Cape Town from KwaZulu Natal in my early twenties. Met a wonderful woman here and we married. Unfortunately, like so many others, we parted ways and before the divorce went through, they murdered her in a hijacking."

"I'm so sorry for your loss. Did they find them?"

"They found the one, but the other had disappeared. Again, like so many others, the docket went missing, and they had to set him free." Thys exhaled a tired breath. "I was angry for a very long time. That's why I opened the gym; to empower anyone willing to learn how to handle themselves in any kind of situation. And so that I could expel pent-up frustration." Thys rubbed his eyes and sat straight in his chair.

"Well, I'm glad Jewel and I found your class. We've learned a lot." I beamed at him.

Thys smiled, and it lit up his face. Our eyes met and something happened between us, something connecting us closer than before, closer than friends. My heartbeat sped up and a nervousness I'd never felt before in his company enveloped me at that moment.

My cellphone beeped, breaking our connection. I glanced away, feeling my cheeks heat, and read the message from Tony, but didn't answer.

When I looked at Thys again, I felt slightly uncomfortable, like I'd just cheated on him by reading a message.

"Let me get the account so that we can go. I think Jewel has homework she still needs to do." I kicked her foot gently under the table so she could agree with me.

The atmosphere shifted, but not in a bad way. I liked Thys, but I liked Tony too. I went from having no one in my life to two men and now I didn't know what to do. The best thing was to do nothing and it would all fall into place the way it was meant to.

The server brought the account after I called him. I paid even though Thys tried to get the account out of my hands. I threatened to hit him in the face again, and he playfully backed down.

"The next one is on me," he said.

"Sure, I'd like that." My smile reached my eyes and I genuinely wanted to see him again.

We left the coffee shop and went our separate ways. As I sat in the front seat of my Ford, I started the engine and watched Thys walk in the other direction. A suspicious man wearing a hoody approached him. They spoke in hushed tones and exchanged a package.

I squinted at what they were doing but couldn't figure out what was in the other man's hands.

"Let's go already, Mom," Jewel said, buckling herself in.

"In a minute," I said, shushing her.

"What are you gawking at." Jewel moved in her seat and I felt her breath on my hand on the steering wheel. "What are they doing? It looks like a drug deal—"

"How do you know what a drug deal looks like?" I asked, frowning.

"Television, Mom. Don't sound so concerned." She tsked and sat back in seat.

"It looks suspicious, doesn't it?"

"It could be perfectly innocent."

"Could be." But I doubted it. Suspicion squashed the feeling I had for Thys, and he became another man I needed to be wary of. We didn't really know Thys either. For all I knew, he could be the killer.

Chapter Nineteen

THE MAN WATCHED Ophelia and Jewel enter the gym. He had at least an hour to do what needed to be done before they came home again.

The man drove past the gym and headed for Ophelia's home, parking around the corner, and approached on foot.

He slipped through the side gate and opened the backdoor without setting off alarms. In South Africa, their only electricity-producing provider had major issues that ranged from having no coal or a complete shutdown of one of their power stations due to maintenance, leaving many South Africans in the dark for six to eight hours a day.

Therefore, load-shedding happened often and sometimes the security features of a home needed electricity to function. Unfortunately, not everyone could afford a backup generator or battery pack, exposing the weak points of the house. Much like this house.

Once inside, the man took his time. He walked through her kitchen and into the open-plan lounge. He smelled her perfume lingering in the air as he imagined her sitting on her couch, sipping on her wine like she did last night.

The man sucked in the air over his teeth as he imagined how she tasted. He closed his eyes and breathed in the air. He wanted more.

The man entered Ophelia's room, adjusted his cock in his pants, and sat on her bed. He fell backwards, arms spread above his head as he imagined Ophelia sleeping beside him. He smelled her pillow and hugged it.

He returned the pillow to its spot, stood up and entered her ensuite bathroom. Her perfume lingered here, too. He opened the cabinet and found nothing interesting. In her shower was nothing of use to him, either.

The man opened her closet and touched her t-shirts and pants. When he found her underwear shelf, he crouched on one knee to get a better look. His long fingers caressed her silk panties and then he picked up a silk bra. He brought the item to his nose and breathed in her scent once more. She was a drug, and he was addicted to her; her movements, her clothing, her scent, *her*.

The man rubbed his eyes and combed his fingers through his unkempt hair. He liked what he saw in Ophelia. She was not like the others. She wasn't as easy or as desperate for attention as the others were. Ophelia was careful, meticulous, and questioned everyone.

He liked Ophelia more as he got to know her.

The man pocketed the items and entered Jewel's room; which was typical for a teenager. Her smell was different, yet similar to her mother's. Jewel was too young. He would not risk his freedom for someone so young and inexperienced.

The man exited Jewel's room and opened the passage closet and found fresh towels, glass bowls, and other knickknacks.

The timer on his watch sounded, and he made his way towards the back door. But before exiting, he opened the fridge. Hungry, the man picked up a block of cheese, unwrapped it, and enjoyed a tiny bite. Next, he stuck his fingers into a spinach and feta quiche; store-bought and not as delicious.

The man opened the freezer section and there were no frozen foods. Feeling a little disappointed, the man closed the doors and exited the house, whistling a tune.

Chapter Twenty

AFTER I SHOWERED AGAIN I dressed in my pajamas. Jewel was in her room watching drawing videos. Although we'd eaten, I was a little peckish and wanted something to eat.

I shivered as I walked through the lounge but it wasn't cold. The hairs on the back of my neck stood on end when I entered the kitchen and I rubbed my arms yet there was no chill in the air.

I switched on the kettle and placed a tea bag in my mug. "Jewel! Do you want some tea?"

"Yes."

"Please," I mumbled under my breath.

"Please," she yelled.

I smiled while opening my fridge and reached for the milk. My eyes darted to the opened cheese. Ice settled in my veins and time passed. My fridge made that annoying noise notifying me to close the door.

"Jewel?"

Silence greeted me.

I closed the fridge and walked to her room. "Jewel, did you take a bite out of the cheese?"

"Huh? No, that's gross, Mom."

"I know, that's why I'm asking." I thought for a moment and rushed to the security keypad. I checked the log, and I never switched it on this morning. The doors were locked, but the alarm wasn't on. I always switched it on. I couldn't understand how I forgot. Unless we had load-shedding while we were at the gym. I'd stopped checking the load-shedding schedule because it frustrated me.

"Jewel, honey, did you switch off the alarm this morning after I turned it on?"

"I was by Dad this morning. You probably forgot with all the things on your mind."

A chill racked my body. I dashed to my cellphone and called Piet.

———

PIET ARRIVED with one police officer within thirty minutes. They checked inside my house, the backyard, and the neighbor's home.

"They broke the side door lock at your neighbor's and we found sweet wrappers near their back door," Piet said, reading his notes. "You should've called me, O. You know I'll help you."

"I know. But I thought it was silly—"

"It's never silly. Trust your intuition. Always." He reprimanded me like one would a child. But he was right. I swallowed hard and nodded. I didn't trust my voice to answer him.

"We'll take the cheese and quiche but doubtful we'll find any saliva or prints. And we'll check the dental records we have on the system." Piet sounded clinical, very matter-of-factly. He'd done this many times and said those words to many victims. "Do you know of anyone who wants to hurt you?"

"No."

"Jewel?"

"What about Jewel?" My eyes flitted to my daughter's room.

"Does anyone want to hurt her?"

"No, she's only fourteen."

"Think, O," he said sternly. "Any new people you've come across the last week or two?"

"Just our new employee." I nervously chewed on my fingernail. "And Eric. We met him at the Thai restaurant last weekend. We showed him some sights on Sunday."

Piet shook his head judgmentally but said nothing. "Can you give me their details so that I can check them out?"

"And can you check Thys—"

"Your self-defense instructor?" I nodded. "Why?" He asked, his brows forming one long bushy eyebrow.

"Last night he met a suspicious character and… it looked weird. So maybe there's something worth pursuing. Maybe? I dunno?"

I gave Piet all the details I had. He checked the house one last time and waited for me to set the alarm before leaving.

Jewel slept in my bed with me but I hardly slept.

Chapter Twenty-One

JACOB AND THOMAS tended to an easy cleaning job while I spent time with Jewel. I wasn't in the right mind frame to clean any scene.

I gave Jewel a sideways hug, leaning my head on her head. She was still a little shorter than me but was growing up fast.

The server greeted us and grabbed menus. We were about to follow her when someone grabbed my waist. I froze. My thoughts darted to Jewel's safety, but I did nothing. As she walked behind the server, all I could do was stare at her leaving as I remained glued to my spot.

"Morning Ophelia," a familiar voice said behind me.

I tried to relax and my fight-or-flight instinct didn't kick in; after years of training with Thys my reflexes froze up on me. This was not good. If someone attacked me from behind, they would've killed me already.

"Are you okay?" He asked, letting go of me and coming into view. Eric smiled charmingly, and it filled me with disgust. I wanted to punch him in the face for grabbing me that way but it was my fault. I should've heard him behind me and I should've stopped him.

My shoulders dropped. My thoughts were everywhere except in the moment. I wasn't paying attention to my surroundings or to my personal safety.

I didn't know what was going on but I needed to sort myself out. I had to focus on my environment to determine whether I was in a safe space or not. With a killer preying on women, I needed to be more careful.

"Hi Eric," I said, trying desperately not to sound irritated. "How are you?" I asked, taking a step away from him.

"Good," he said. His smile wilting. "Are you okay?"

"Sorry, I've had a rough week." I started walking away from him. "Jewel is waiting for me." I pointed to where she sat and felt awful for dismissing him but I needed space after the fright he'd given me.

"Would you mind if I joined you?" He asked close behind me. "The coffee shop is busy, and it seems you two have the last table."

I stopped walking and my eyes flitted around the room. He was right. We had taken the last available table. I wanted to say 'no, you can't join us', but I didn't want to be rude and turn him away. My folks taught me manners and that declining a friend in need was wrong, especially if I could help. And the table was big enough for four.

"Sure," I said begrudgingly.

"Great." Eric placed his hand on the small of my back and I quickened my step so that I was out of his grasp.

I sat beside Jewel who looked surprised to see Eric.

Eric sat across from us and smiled sweetly at the server as he ordered his drink. My eyes flitted from his mouth as he spoke to his hands holding the menu, particularly the right pinkie finger missing the top part. He didn't seem bothered that I was staring.

Jewel and I ordered our drinks and busied ourselves reading the menu we knew well.

"Think I'll just have a toasted sandwich," Eric said, placing his menu down. "Thanks for letting me join you. If you don't mind me asking. What happened this week that has you so rattled?" His piercing dark eyes unsettled me.

"Someone murdered my best friend, and someone broke into our house." My words were clipped and my tone harsh.

"My condolences." Eric glanced at his hands as he continued speaking. "I lost someone long ago, and it still hurts." When he looked up his eyes held unshed tears. "I hope they find the killer. And catch the person who broke into your home."

I sighed weakly. Everybody had a story to tell, but it was how we treated others that also mattered. I could be miserable for the rest of my life and not trust anybody, or I could mourn the loss of my friend and still be compassionate towards others.

"I'm sorry to hear of your loss," I said. "I guess we've all lost loved ones."

Jewel grabbed my hand under the table, and it comforted me.

"How about we change the subject?" Jewel asked, squeezing my hand.

I was being selfish and had forgotten about Jewel's feelings and what she was going through. I squeezed her hand back but didn't let go.

"Agreed," I said, beaming lovingly at my child. "Tell us about work. Did you succeed in what you wanted to accomplish in the Cape?"

"Yes, the international company I met with is happy to merge with mine. The paperwork has already started and I'll fly back to Joburg next week." He leaned back in the chair. The silence stretched between us.

"But before I leave there's something I've wanted to do," he continued. "I've hiked all over the world but never in my own country so I'd like to hike here," — he circled a finger in the air, — "and I was wondering whether the two of you would like to join me. You're welcome to bring anyone else along. I've heard there have been attacks on some of the hiking trails so the more the merrier."

"Do you have a specific hiking trail in mind?" I asked, sipping on the cappuccino the server brought.

"I heard the forest at Echo Valley in Muizenberg is magnificent. I just need to get a hiking bag." Eric sipped on his coffee. "Do you have a bag?"

"We have a small backpack or two that we could use." I glanced at Jewel who nodded in agreement.

The server brought our food, and we started eating.

"Would you be able to hike tomorrow? My plane leaves early on Tuesday so I really only have tomorrow left." Eric ate a forkful of his food and hummed as he chewed. He seemed to be in a good mood.

"It should be ok. But if a cleaning job pops up, we'll have to cancel."

Jewel squeezed my hand. I didn't think she wanted to go, but I didn't want to go alone and I didn't want to be rude to Eric either. Eric had done nothing to cause alarm, but with the break-in yesterday, I didn't want to take the chance.

"No problem. Should I see you there, rather? That way, if you need to leave, you can."

"Sounds good. I'll see if my cleaning team can join us.

We have a new employee, and this would be a good way for us to get to know him."

"How many employees do you have?"

"For now just two."

Eric nodded while he chewed and listened. "Is your business doing well?" He asked while concentrating on his knife and fork skills. Jewel and I used our hands to eat our toasted sandwich yet Eric cut small bites with his utensils.

"Yes, we do all right. We could get more business if I advertised but right now we're busy enough."

"Good," Eric said, smiling. "I hope you don't mind if I eat and run. I have a few things to take care of and then buy a few items for the hike tomorrow."

"Sure, no problem." I smiled as I watched Eric finish his food in record time. At least Jewel and I could finish our meal without further interruptions.

Eric left some of his chips on his plate, left cash on the table to pay for his food, and stood up.

"Is 8 a.m. good with you?" Eric asked.

"Yep, 8 is perfect. We'll see you there."

When Eric left I sent a message to Jacob and Thomas, inviting them for a hike.

Chapter Twenty-Two

THE MAN frustratingly combed his fingers through his oily hair. He pulled on his collar so he could breathe easily but no matter what he did; he remained frustrated and uncomfortable.

This wasn't how it should be. His date had called saying she would be late and to order her a drink while he waited for her. Instead of him watching her through the restaurant window like he always did, he sat at the table waiting for her.

He twisted the napkin in his hands until it hurt. When the server approached with his drink, he carefully placed the napkin in his lap. The man graciously accepted the drink, downed the contents, and ordered another one.

The man never waited for his prey. He always waited and watched them, assessing them, picking up their mannerisms; something he could never do in their online chats. He had to watch them first before walking through the restaurant door. Yet this female had seemed meek and mild online and had stood him up for reasons unknown.

The man wondered whether she had noticed him waiting outside the restaurant and decided against meeting him, making up an excuse not to go through with the date.

Whatever her reason was, it wasn't a good sign. The man needed to know why she didn't want to meet him. Or, he needed to find her and teach her a lesson for making him wait.

Nobody made him wait. *No one.*

But the man knew little about her. She was careful in her responses to him. She didn't leave hints of where her home was or the places she frequently visited. And she wasn't on any social media.

He exhaled a frustrated breath and rubbed his face. His eyes flitted across the room and the lines between his eyes deepened. The place was empty for a Saturday night. He'd never seen it with so few patrons before.

Not wanting to wait around like prey himself, the man left the rose and cash on the table, then darted for the door.

As he reached for the handle, a nervousness he hadn't felt before made him glance over his shoulder. He saw his server speaking with a large man wearing a hoody.

The man glanced out the glass door at his car and one other. Otherwise, the parking lot was eerily empty. He didn't hesitate and headed for the bathroom, locking the door behind him. There was a reason he only came to this restaurant. It was one of the few in the city that had a working tunnel beneath it.

Apart from a drawing of the tunnels printed on the menu, it was unknown that this restaurant still had direct access to working tunnels. The man had researched the venue well. He'd found the plans and layout of the building in order to plan an exit strategy if he needed to escape. It relieved him that his due diligence had panned out.

The man surmised the owners of the restaurant had illegally reopened the secret doorway that led down to the tunnels. He understood that most accesses were closed by the city to ensure vagrants didn't settle down there. He doubted they used it for anything nefarious but it was something they could market if business died down.

During his investigation, the man had discovered the restaurant was a brothel in the sixties. The public knew it as a men-only pub called Milk and Whiskey. They had used the tunnels to transport prostitutes unseen by the public and had built an access doorway in the men's bathroom.

The underground tunnels of Cape Town dated back as far as 1652. They first began as canals transporting millions of liters of fresh spring water from Table Mountain directly out to sea. Today, tourists used the tunnels, so slipping down from the men's utility closet down a man-hole; the man could confidently blend in with the tourists.

The man quietly opened the door, and a musky smell assaulted his nose. He wrinkled his nose and then quietly jumped down into a puddle of murky water making a soft splash sound. A cockroach scuttled across the floor and into a crack in the wall.

Water dripped down the sides of the tunnel. Moss covered small areas on the floor and wall. And although the tunnel was dark, he could see without a flashlight.

Sounds up ahead of indistinct murmurs and laughter caught the man's attention. He glanced left and right, then headed in the sound's direction.

Chapter Twenty-Three

THE MAN GREETED the last of the tourists as they exited the tunnels. As he rounded the corner, he glanced at the tour guide, who stared suspiciously at him. When a woman asked the tour guide a question, the man used the opportunity and ran up the steep incline towards the streets above.

Fixing his shirt, the man wrinkled his nose; the smell of the tunnel lingering. He crossed the street and headed back towards the restaurant.

He traversed along the quiet sidewalk; the only sounds came from cars driving past. As the man neared the restaurant, red and blue lights flashed against the white shop walls and between the trees. Police cars swarmed the area with enough arms and ammunition for a small war.

The man blended in with the shadows as he watched the large police officer shine a light inside his vehicle; a car that belonged to nobody. The police officer searched the front seat but found nothing they could trace back to him.

The police officer asked someone to assist him; they

checked the backseat and the trunk while another person checked under the hood for the engine number.

The police officer turned around, and the man noticed the dark hoody, it was similar to the man who had been speaking with the restaurant server earlier.

The man silently cursed himself; he needed to be more careful. The woman he'd been speaking with online was undercover. She had lured him to this restaurant under false pretenses and he doubted she was even a woman, but the police officer searched his vehicle.

Chapter Twenty-Four

THOMAS FETCHED Jacob and met us at my house at seven. We loaded our hiking backpacks into the back of my Ford, buckled in, and headed towards Echo Valley in Muizenberg.

The forty-minute drive to Echo Valley was scenic with sea views and minimal traffic since it was early on a Sunday morning. I parked the vehicle close to the start of the hiking trail, and everyone silently climbed out and retrieved their backpacks from the back.

Jacob removed his jersey and threw it into the back seat; in the years I'd known Jacob, I'd never noticed the scar on his neck. Ever since Piet mentioned they'd profiled the killer as an intelligent man with the possibility of having a disfigurement, I noticed things I hadn't before.

I was seeing scars and imperfections on men I wouldn't normally and couldn't help but wonder if they were the killer. I obviously had my doubts. There was no way Jacob could be the killer. It just proved that profiling a killer was so generic and widespread that it could be anyone; the killer could be any one of us. Most of us had scars or limps, or some type of flaw.

I stared at my hands and they were dry from all the cleaning. I needed to take better care of myself.

"You made it," Eric said behind me and I flinched... again. I had to get a grip. "Hi, I'm Eric," he said, shaking hands with Jacob and Thomas.

I grabbed my backpack from Jewel, who stood close to me. "How are you?" I asked, but before he answered, he hugged me and then Jewel, who gave him a sideways hug.

"I'm great." He sucked in a deep breath and exhaled. "I mean, just smell all that fresh air. I really love it out here." He smiled and something twinkled in his eyes. "I'm even thinking of moving my business this side. Most of my employees work remotely, so it wouldn't matter where I lived or where the main office was."

"Yes," I said, smiling and glancing up at the mountain we were about to hike. "It is lovely here with much to do. We have the beach, mountains, wine, delicious food and so many activities. And I agree, after COVID no company should force any employee to come into the office. If working remotely during COVID worked, why not allow them to stay at home."

"Except you guys," Eric said, chuckling. "You, unfortunately, need to go to the places."

"Yeah, unfortunately, we need to travel. But it's what we chose to do."

The silence stretched uncomfortably as we stared at each other. Birds called behind us while cars passed by.

"Should we get started?" I asked, breaking the silence.

"A friend of mine who hikes often sent me a map we could follow if you like," Eric said, pulling out his phone and tapping on the screen. He showed me an app featuring a path going directly to the forest area I enjoyed visiting. "It connects to a satellite. If there's no cellphone signal we'll still be able to find our way."

"Cool, thanks for organizing."

"No problem. Right, are we ready?" Eric asked, looking around. We nodded in unison. "Good, this way," Eric said enthusiastically, pointing to the left and walked in that direction.

I walked behind Eric with Jewel behind me. Thomas and Jacob were chatting at the back like old friends, laughing at various jokes. It relieved me they were getting along. The last thing I wanted was for my colleagues to fight, and create an unpleasant environment for all.

It was only after thirty minutes when the guys in the back became silent. We traversed along the worn path up the mountain and I was grateful it wasn't steep and Eric was going at a leisurely pace.

I inhaled a deep breath, catching the smells of the various wild plants and flowers growing near the path. I stopped and looked at the men behind us. The view of the cobalt-blue sea against the sky was breathtaking. Eric and Jewel stopped, and we enjoyed the view and the fresh air.

In the distance was the Hottentots-Holland Mountains Catchment area, and on the other side was Simon's Town. No matter which way we looked, the beautiful landscape captured our attention.

"It's really beautiful here," Eric said, barely out of breath.

My chest ached a little. It had been a while since I hiked and nodded breathlessly.

"Let's carry on," Eric said. "I don't want to be out for too long in the blistering sun."

I glanced up at the rocky mountain; the heat beating

down on my face. It was a very warm winter day; which rarely happened. "Give me a second," I yelled. "Just need to put on sunscreen."

I sprayed the sunscreen on Jewel's arms and she rubbed it in herself and I did the same. Then we added some to our faces, pulled on a cap, and enjoyed a sip of cold water before we got heatstroke.

When I looked again, Eric was in the distance, calling us over. "We're here," he yelled and disappeared.

We quickened our steps and reached the entrance to the majestic forest. The cool shade of the trees was a welcomed sensation against my hot skin.

Eric sat on one of the wooden benches with a silly grin on his face. "Beautiful, isn't it?"

"Yes, it's stunning."

Eric jumped up and continued up the wooden path that slithered between the trees.

"Should we rest over here?" Eric said, pointing at a large open spot under the trees.

"Sure," I said and reached for Jewel's hand. "Are you hungry?"

"Uh-huh," she said, smiling.

"Tired?"

"Just a little. At least it's beautiful here," Jewel said, choosing a place to sit far away from Eric. She unclipped her rolled-up mat and sat on it.

I removed my mat and sat beside her. The ground was damp and covered in leaves. We placed our backpacks behind us after taking out our sandwiches and bottles of water. We leaned against our backpacks and enjoyed our snacks.

Jacob and Thomas sat on the other side of Jewel. When I wanted to offer Eric some almonds, he had moved closer to the wooden steps that curved around the tree branches and went up before the steps disappeared behind a large rock.

"Would you like to join us?" I said. "We're sharing our snacks."

"No thanks," Eric said. His smile was kind, but the look in his eyes told me otherwise; I wondered whether he felt like the odd one out. There was nothing I could do to make him feel welcome other than what I'd already done.

"Fritos?" Thomas asked, holding out a packet of the tomato flavored chips.

"No thanks. Almonds?"

"Thanks." Thomas held out his hand, and I poured some into his palm. He smiled as he chewed the nuts. He offered chips to Eric, but he declined, then Thomas sat on the other side of Jacob, settling in as he ate the rest of the nuts and chips.

"This is nice, Miss Ophelia," Jacob said, holding his hand up and shaking his head. "I'm not a fan of any kind of nut."

"It is nice." I lowered the hand holding the packet of nuts and enjoyed another bite. "And I'm glad it worked out that we could enjoy a Sunday off. We haven't had a Sunday off in a while."

"Umm-hmm," Jacob hummed as he chewed his sandwich. "We've all needed a break. It's been a long, busy year."

I couldn't agree more with him.

Sounds of people talking and feet stomping on the weathered wooden steps neared as more hikers entered the forest. They greeted us and continued up the path until we no longer heard them.

Eric moved again and sat on the other side of the

wooden path with his back against a large rock, eating his pasta salad. He stretched his legs out in front of him and pressed his head against the rock and stared up at the trees while he chewed.

My eyes flitted to his pinkie finger, missing the tip, and wondered what had happened.

"Butcher's accident," Eric said, bringing me out of my thoughts.

"Excuse me?"

"The finger," — he wiggled his pinkie, — "I was six when playing in my uncle's butcher shop. The guillotine fell and chopped the tip off. I remember it fell into the container they were filling to make sausage and before I could get it out, it joined the rest of the meat and got minced." He fell quiet for a moment, then added, "I didn't tell them where it went. Only that it was gone. They stitched me together, and I was back in the butcher's shop the next day. This time I kept my fingers off the counter."

I didn't know what to say, so I kept quiet. I couldn't understand how anybody could leave a six-year-old alone to play with sharp knives. I wasn't there and didn't know the circumstances. It was my impression that meat guillotines had strong handles and didn't just fall.

Eric finished his salad and stuffed his empty container back into his backpack and sank lower until he was on his back, staring up at the trees.

Jewel finished her trail mix of nuts, seeds, and cranberries. She enjoyed a few sips of her water and rested on her backpack.

Jacob and Thomas were already asleep.

I finished my snack and laid down. The air was cool against my skin, and the trees above us moved slightly as a breeze blew through the branches. I closed my eyes and allowed my senses to enjoy the moment. The sounds of birds and the branches scraping against the other soothed my racing heart. The smell of wet ground assaulted my olfactory senses, yet pleasant enough not to block my nose.

I absorbed the sounds and smells as my mind took me to calm waters with animals drinking. The landscape was magnificent, and the sunset was breathtaking. Lucy was there. Her smile was contagious. Her red hair moved gently in the breeze. She stood between a boulder and an old tree with branches that reached high above the boulder.

I'd never seen Lucy so happy before. Her skin was pale and her eyes were almost translucent. Her smile turned upside down as her skin peeled off her body. Blood oozed out of the fresh wounds and dripped down her chest and legs, pooling at her feet. Her hands cupped her cheeks as she screamed silently. Blood tears dripped from her eyes and down her cheeks. Then her body decomposed, leaving nothing but chunks of flesh and green slime everywhere.

A twig snapped behind me and I jerked awake, sitting upright. My pulse thundered in my ears and my chest ached. I sucked in deep breaths of air while searching for Lucy. But she was gone; it was only a dream.

"Where's Jewel?" Jacob asked, coming into my line of sight.

"Huh? What?" I glanced to my right, and it was only her backpack beside me. "Where is she?"

"Not sure. We fell asleep and when I woke up, she was already gone." Jacob stepped onto the wooden path, walked towards the boulder Eric was sitting against, and returned. "Eric is gone, too." A nervousness I'd never seen in Jacob before left me unsettled.

I bolted to my feet. "Jewel!" I yelled and ran up the wooden path. "Jewel? Where are you?" I ran around the boulder where Eric had been, finding the ground disturbed. "Oh my gods," I breathed. "Where is she?" I said to myself more than anyone else.

I hugged my arms. My veins filled with dread at the thought of Jewel hurt and bleeding somewhere alone. Her backpack was undisturbed; she'd gotten up and left. There weren't any scuff marks on the ground either; no one had dragged her away.

I glanced at Jacob and where he was sleeping beside Thomas, in the large vacant space. "Where's Thomas?"

"He needed the bathroom."

I ran down the wooden path, searching both sides for any movement. When I reached the end of the wooden path and saw another hiking group heading our way, I turned around and ran up the path, the steep steps that curved around a rock, I ducked under tree branches but not low enough as one twig scraped my cheek.

I bolted up the path towards a cave, and visions of finding my baby girl filled me with dread. She was mine; losing a child was every parent's worst nightmare. I imagined the colorful language her father would use when I gave him the news that his baby was gone. That someone had murdered our child when I was meant to protect her.

I shook my head in shame for falling asleep, for leaving my child alone, for not protecting her. She could protect herself, but there was a killer out there. He could easily hurt her; one hit to the head could incapacitate anyone.

I closed the distance with the cave-like structure, but it was only a large rock that sat to one side and created shelter.

To my left, I heard murmurs and squinted in that direction, and then something moved. My heart lodged in my throat and I couldn't breathe. *Jewel?*

"Jewel?" I called softly, squinting in the distance. I wanted the blur to be her. I needed it to be her, but I was afraid it might be someone or something else. "Jewel," I said louder. I traversed through the dense brush, pushing branches out of my way, and headed in the direction I saw the movement.

The murmurs became words I understood, and my pace quickened.

I stopped at a bush with red berries and watched Eric explain to Jewel the differences between edible ones and those that were poisonous.

"Didn't you hear me yelling?" I said, trying to catch my breath. My throat was dry, and I gripped my pants to stop the shaking.

Jewel stared guiltily at me. "Sorry. I went to the bathroom and, on my way back, I bumped into Eric. He knows a lot about nature."

"I can see that." My tone was sharp. "Why didn't you wake me?"

"You were sleeping—"

"I don't care," I yelled. "Wake me next time. I need to know where you are." The lines between my eyes deepened. "Come, I want to go home."

"Sorry," Eric said. "It's my fault. I didn't think you'd mind if I explained a few things to Jewel." He sounded remorseful, but something in his facial features contradicted his words, leaving me confused. "There's so much beauty here I had to share." He raised his arms and pointed at the beautiful rock formation and entwined trees.

I agreed with his sentiment and sighed. "It's fine. I just got a fright, that's all."

Eric fidgeted with his shirt, quickly tucking it in. The top of his hands had scratch marks that could've been from branches.

"Let's go." Eric jerked his chin in the path's direction. "It's getting hot out in the sun and doubt we want to be stuck here all afternoon."

Eric guided Jewel towards the path, and I followed. He glanced over his shoulder at me, as if sensing my dark stare.

Chapter Twenty-Five

"WHERE WERE YOU?" I said, staring at Thomas' dirty shirt. "It looks like you were fighting in the dirt."

Thomas dusted his hands on his shirt, but all that did was make it dirtier.

"I finished using the outdoor bathroom, turned and tripped over a rock," — he held up his scratched palms, — "then I got lost, going out of the forest and going downhill. That's when I realized I was too far out and turned around, coming back up the path we had used earlier." He thumbed over his shoulder at the path behind him.

Thomas combed his fingers through his hair, leaving it standing in all directions. Sweat dripped down the sides of his sand-marked face. His smaller ear had a deep cut that had already started caking.

"Are you ready to leave?" I asked, picked up my backpack and stuffed the empty wrappers in a side pocket.

Thomas nodded and grabbed his backpack.

Jacob stood beside me, ready.

Jewel moved around me to pack her things and pulled

on her backpack. She avoided eye contact as she traversed around Thomas and Jacob, putting distance between us.

I felt guilty for yelling at Jewel, but I got a fright. I'd wait for the dust to settle before I said anything. We could talk about the events when we got home.

Eric led the way back down the mountain. We followed him in silence. I was exhausted and miserable.

We reached the vehicles a few minutes after two in the afternoon. We'd been out on the mountain for almost six hours. It felt like we were in the forest for only a few minutes, but it was at least two hours.

"Thanks for joining me today," Eric said, smiling.

"It was fun," I said and closed the gap. We hugged and I quickly let go.

Eric greeted Jacob and Thomas with a stern handshake and waved at Jewel. I suspected he didn't want me seeing red again and I appreciated the thought.

We stood watching Eric climb into his black luxury vehicle and drive off.

"I need the bathroom," Jewel said with a pained expression.

"Let's go. I saw a place nearby."

We ordered drinks at a restaurant near the hiking trail. We freshened up in their bathrooms and found a table with ocean and street views.

When our coffee and cake arrived, the first police car sped past. I sipped the hot liquid and flinched when another car with a loud siren drove past. Then an ambulance. Then, a white forensic pathologist van.

"I wonder what happened?" Jacob said.

"I don't know," I said, sipping my coffee.

We watched another car drive past like watching a live-action movie. I could still see the blue and red lights from their cars.

"They're close—" Jewel mumbled.

"Like they're by the hiking trail." My words didn't sink in until I recognized the last vehicle zooming by.

I stood up, leaned over the table, and pressed my face against the glass. All the vehicles blocked the road while point-men directed traffic to turn around.

"They are by the hiking trail. Something happened." What I didn't say was something might have happened while we were there. And we had just missed it. "Let's finish. I want to chat with Piet."

Chapter Twenty-Six

I PAID THE BILL, and we walked up the road back towards the start of the hiking trail.

A police officer stopped us and told us to go back.

"Can you call Detective Piet for me, please?"

He narrowed his eyes. "Sorry, ma'am, he's busy."

"It's important. Or I can phone him and tell him you aren't doing your job."

The police officer scowled, then reluctantly called Piet over the radio.

"Who is it?" Piet asked, his voice crackling over the speaker.

"No idea, but she's pushy."

I smiled at the police officer. "It's Ophelia," I said loudly.

"Okay, okay, I'm on my way."

"See," I said, grinning. "That wasn't so difficult."

The officer rolled his eyes and pointed. "Stand to one side while you wait for the detective, please."

"Thank you."

We did as asked and sat on the sidewalk behind the last police vehicle.

"I've never seen you so assertive, Mom," Jewel said beside me, wearing a matching grin.

"Why thank you, little one. I hope you're learning."

"O, what are you doing here?" Piet said, out of breath. His sweat-drenched shirt clung to his body and his face was red from running.

I licked dry lips and stood up. "We were just there, Piet."

"What do you mean?" Piet asked, thumbing behind him. "You were on the trail?"

"Yes, we exited the trail about thirty minutes ago. We were sitting in the coffee shop around the corner when you all flew in here like bats out of hell."

We stared at each other knowingly. Piet glanced at Jewel, then back at me. The victim could've been either of us.

I glanced at Thomas, who had washed his hands and face in the bathroom. The scrapes on his hands and palms were still visible from his fall. He caught me staring, but I didn't care. I didn't really know him and suspected everyone. There was a killer on the mountain, and it frightened me. I trusted no one when it came to the safety of me and my daughter.

"Did you see anything?" Piet asked seriously. "Anything suspicious?"

I saw nothing, but Thomas and Eric had disappeared for a short while. And even though Eric spoke with Jewel for some of the time, we didn't know him either.

"No, I saw nothing," I said. "We saw another hiking group pass ours. We were in the forest area taking a break when they came through."

Piet nodded as he scribbled something in his notebook.

"Did you find another body?" I whispered. I didn't want Jewel to hear, even though she was close enough.

He nodded but said nothing.

"Is it the same killer targeting women?"

He narrowed his eyes. But he knew me. I wouldn't stop with the questions until I got some kind of answer. "We don't know. Maybe."

"Why?"

"You know I can't say anything."

"Please."

"We know little, but a hiker discovered the body of a female hiker. The killer left markings similar to the other victims. We will know more when the coroner completes his investigation. For now," — Piet said, squeezing my shoulder, — "go home." His eyes flitted to Jewel who had stepped closer and heard. I couldn't protect her from what was going on. She was bound to hear it, eventually.

I swallowed the lump in my throat and reached for Jewel to stand closer, threading my arm with hers.

"Where was her body found?"

"On the other side of the forest."

"There was no one else except us," — I pointed at us, — "and Eric."

"If you remember anything else, call me. I need to go. Take care of yourself."

"Thanks, Piet."

Piet nodded curtly, spun around, and ran back to his colleagues.

Chapter Twenty-Seven

THE RIDE HOME WAS QUIET, apart from the sounds of the engine and tires.

Thomas avoided making eye contact with me. Jacob used his phone the entire ride back while Jewel fell asleep; at least one of us was relaxed enough to sleep.

When I parked the vehicle inside my driveway, Thomas bolted out of the car, waving as he greeted us without glancing our way, with Jacob following closely behind him.

"See you tomorrow morning, Miss Ophelia," Jacob said, waving as he ran to catch up with Thomas.

"Bye," I said and closed the gate behind them.

I sighed wearily. I didn't know what to do. I didn't know if I could trust Thomas. At first, he seemed fine, but after today his behavior seemed strange. I wasn't so sure anymore.

"Are you okay?" Jewel asked beside me, wrapping her arm around my waist and leaning her head on my shoulder.

"Yeah."

"Today was strange."

"Yep." I kissed the top of her head. "Let's not dwell on it. What we need is dinner and lots of it. What are we having?"

"That's your job." She glanced up with a grin. "Whatever it is, they must deliver it. I don't feel like going anywhere else now. My feet hurt and I smell. I may even have blisters." She stared down at her shoes. "And these are my comfy sneakers."

"Definitely delivery. I don't want to leave the house until tomorrow." I sighed again. "And your dad is picking you up before school in the morning."

She groaned with her cheek back on my shoulder. "Do I have to?" She let go of me and headed for the house.

"It's your dad's turn to have you for the week, Jewel."

"I know…" she mumbled something I didn't hear but left it. Whatever she was going through, she needed to deal with it on her own. Unless she needed my help, I was confident she'd ask for my help when the time came. If she had an issue with her father, she had to speak with him about it.

My cellphone pinged; it was another message from Tony.

"Hey, are you still up for a coffee date tomorrow morning?"

I'd completely forgotten about that. My thumb hovered over the letter 'N'; at the moment, my head wasn't anywhere near coffee or dating. Then I felt guilty for cancelling on him the last time.

"Sure," I typed, agreeing to meet him at the coffee shop on Beach Road after Will fetched Jewel. My thinking was if anything happened to me, I was within walking distance of Will's shop. I doubted it would help much, but it was comforting in case something went wrong.

"I'm getting burgers," I yelled as I entered the front door, closed it, and bolted it shut. I turned on the alarm and headed for Jewel's room. "Which burger do you feel like?" I asked as I entered her bedroom and stopped dead.

My brain performed a somersault of sorts at the sight before me. I blinked and closed my mouth, licking dry lips a second time today. I swallowed hard and stepped back. My eyes flitted from the scene to Jewel, who stood motionless.

"Jewel, get out now," I said, reaching for her hand. "I'm calling Piet."

Chapter Twenty-Eight

I HUGGED Jewel tightly until she double-tapped my shoulder. "Can't breathe, Mom," she said, smiling. It relieved me to see that smile and that she was no longer crying.

"I think she must stay with you until they find this creep," I said to Will, who nodded. He had the common decency to leave his new bride at home; this was our family business. He was welcome to tell her everything when he got home but the last thing I needed now was another woman commenting on our business. "I'll transfer some cash for petrol and food."

"It's okay," Will said, holding Jewel's hand.

"Oh?" My eyebrows raised.

"A big order of surfboards came through with the possibility of them becoming repeat clients." He grinned. I hadn't seen him happy like this since the day I told him I was pregnant.

I beamed at him. "Congratulations, you must be relieved."

"Of course. And this client is quite influential and might refer my business to his friends and clients." He was quiet for a moment, then added, "You know, I don't always want to take your money, Ophelia." He sounded genuine.

It was the first time in a really long while that I didn't want to gouge out Will's eyes. He was usually pleasant to hang around and spoke to me with respect. But after the divorce and his cheating on me with a string of women, our relationship had suffered. But right now I couldn't help but smile at his latest achievement.

I hugged Jewel one last time and gave Will her bag. "Call me any time and I'll pop around tomorrow after my cleaning job." I kissed Jewel on the cheek and swallowed the lump in my throat, watching them walk to Will's car.

"We'll catch him, O," Piet said behind me.

"Do you know how he gained entrance?"

"Your bathroom window."

I frowned and turned around.

"We think he used a crowbar to pull your burglar bars out of the wall and climbed through. And it happened recently. Probably right before you got home."

Ice filled my veins. It wasn't Thomas; he was with us in the car during that time and Jacob was with him thereafter. He didn't have time to break open my bathroom window, kill our neighbor's cat and leave it on Jewel's bed.

"What does it mean?" I asked, thumbing my house behind me. "Why leave a dead cat?"

"It's not so much the animal he killed, but what he left inside the chest cavity."

My frown deepened.

"Remember when you cleaned that one crime scene in the beginning and found the necklace—"

"Yes," I said, my palms becoming sweaty. "I remember."

The silver necklace with a ruby in the middle of a silver rose.

"It seems he has a bunch of them." Piet rubbed his face and red blotches marked his cheeks. I doubted he'd been home in a while. His red-rimmed eyes hadn't slept yet and there was stubble along his jawline.

"Are you working around the clock?"

"Yeah, this has been a tough one, O." Piet sounded deflated. Exhausted. "I've had enough. But I won't rest until we have him."

"There are no fingerprints, Detective," one of the police officers said as he exited the house. He pulled off his gloves and combed his damp, spiky hair. "He left nothing except what we found on the bed."

"Have you removed it?" Piet asked.

"Yes, Detective. We cleared the scene, and it's ready for cleaning."

I almost laughed at the irony; at least I had the chemicals to clean Jewel's room properly. I'd first discard her mattress, then clean any dried blood found on the floor.

"Thanks, Deon. Is everyone ready to leave?"

"Yes, Detective. They're just picking up all the shards of glass for testing," Deon said, shrugging. "Maybe they'll find a print on one of them." He sighed and rubbed his bloodshot eyes. It was clear the case was taking its toll on everybody.

"Good. Do you know if the labs are done with the previous items?" Piet asked.

"No, there's still a backlog."

"I'll phone them to speed things up. I'll see you at the station."

Deon tipped his head in confirmation and stalked to his vehicle, which stood outside and behind all the others.

Before he climbed into his white van, he picked up the black body bag holding the poor cat and placed it in the back. He waved at us as we watched him climb in and drive away.

"Do you think the killer uses the necklace to entice his victims?" I said absentmindedly. "You've only seen this necklace at two scenes, or did he leave them at all the crime scenes?"

"Only the two. And I think it's something special to him. We had the first one researched, and it's an expensive piece. We'll have this one tested too. I think the killer is too good for costume jewelry."

"Hmm," I said, thinking. "Why is he letting us know it's him who is stalking me and that he's the Lady Killer?"

"He wants the recognition. He's proud of what he's done and rubbing it in our faces that we haven't caught him yet." Piet shook his head in disappointment. "And he'll keep doing it until we finally stop him."

My mouth was dry again. The thought of this man following me or any woman was frightening.

"Do you think he's proud of what he's done?"

"Of course," Piet said, appearing shocked I asked such a stupid question. "He wants us to know how good he is. There's no evidence linking anyone to the scenes. Like Deon has said the lab is behind. I can only hope they find something. But…" Piet left his word hanging as he thought of something.

A knot formed in the pit of my stomach and something told me that whatever came out of his mouth next might spell disaster for me.

Piet stared at me; his glassy-colored blue eyes had lost their sparkle but clutched onto an idea.

"He's watching you, O. And if I had to guess, this guy will do whatever he can to get you."

I giggled nervously, but it fell flat as the magnitude of his words sunk in.

"He's watching you," Piet repeated in a whisper.

I looked around and saw no one. My nervous laugh was back. I didn't know how to respond.

"We can't go after him without evidence. We don't know who he is, and we can't afford to wait around for him to make a mistake. I doubt he'll ever make a mistake, unless…"

"Unless what?"

Piet stared hard at me, willing me to read his mind.

"No," I said, shaking my head. "You're crazy. I cannot do that."

"Let him come to you and we'll be waiting for him." Piet's words were barely above a whisper.

I stared dumbfounded at him.

Chapter Twenty-Nine

"I'LL BE FINE. I'm safe. Nobody will hurt me…" I said to myself repeatedly as I paced in my living room.

"We're all set," Piet said, making me flinch. "It's okay, O, I promise. I will protect you with my life." His words were comforting, but the thought of having a killer after me left me rattled.

Piet smiled and gave me a thumbs up as he sheathed a knife to my belt. I moved the belt to the left so that it wouldn't dig into my back.

"Do you know how to use it?"

"Yes, Thys has shown us how to use various items as weapons against an attacker."

"Good. More women need to attend self-defense classes. Ladies are much smaller and weaker——" he raised his hands in surrender when I scowled at him. "I only mean that men can hurt ladies easier. Some are tough, but most can't handle themselves."

I knew Piet was correct, but I didn't have to agree with everything he said.

Chapter Thirty

THE MAN GLARED over his sunglasses frames, squinted, and then pushed the frames up his nose. He leaned back in his chair, folded his arms across his chest, and waited.

When the first police siren cut through the quiet air, a grin stretched his face. He leaned forward, gripped the steering wheel and watched police vehicle after vehicle fly past him.

The man didn't think they'd find the body on the hiking trail so quickly but was relieved it happened while he could watch.

When Ophelia darted out of the coffee shop with her daughter, the man smiled. "There you are," he mumbled to himself. It amazed him she didn't discover the body herself since he was so close.

He started the engine, placed the car into first gear and slowly drove into traffic, watching Ophelia speak with the detective. The man grinned as he thought of an idea.

He wanted Ophelia alone. He knew the police would

watch her. They would try to protect her. But he'd be waiting.

Chapter Thirty-One

I RARELY CHEWED on my bottom lip, but I seemed to be doing it often now. My clothing clung to my body like a second skin and my cheeks burned. I pulled my top away from my chest and fanned myself.

"Keep still," Piet said into my earpiece.

"Easy for you to say. You aren't the bait."

Piet chuckled in my ear, coughed, and then quickly added, *"I'm near to you, O. My boys and I will do everything in our power to keep you safe. I promise."*

My arms pebbled. "I know." I sighed wearily. "I still don't like the situation I'm in."

"Understandably," Piet said. There were muffled voices in the background, and then he added, *"I know it's hard, but try to relax we're struggling to hear you."*

I wanted to yell at him that relaxing was impossible. A serial killer was targeting women, and he had his sights on me. Relaxing was not on my mind.

I shuddered at the thought and swallowed hard when I remembered Lucy; we could've prevented her senseless death. This was the reason I was putting my life on the line; to stop his killing spree. I wouldn't be able to live with myself if he murdered another woman.

I sat cross-legged on the couch and stared vacantly out of the curtain-less window. The blinds in my kitchen were wide open, and I felt the gaze of the police officers staring at me from all sides.

I was alone in my house; Jewel was safe with her father, with a police officer watching over them. The killer couldn't go after anyone else.

Piet thought it best to provide the illusion of being home alone. But right now, the air felt thick and suffocating with so many people surrounding me.

I jumped up from the couch and opened a window, the breeze was cool against my skin.

Piet had said that including a civilian in an ongoing investigation happened rarely, but because the killer had specifically targeted me, Piet's boss had given the go ahead along with resources to ensure my safety. I was only seeing a part of what Piet and his men did, and it was scary, yet they did this every day. I didn't know how they stayed sane.

"Going to make myself some tea. Would anyone like?" I said to nobody in particular, but Piet laughed into my ear again.

"How about we enjoy a drink when this is over."

"Deal," I said and switched on the kettle.

———

I JERKED AWAKE. The book I'd been reading crashed to the floor, but not before hitting the plate and messing mustard everywhere.

The house was dark, and muffled sounds echoed in my

ear. I rubbed my eyes and stood up. I flicked on the light switch and waited for my eyes to adjust to the brightness of my lounge.

"I guess he ain't showing tonight," I said into the ether and yawned.

"We aren't going anywhere," Piet said, then spoke in Afrikaans to his men. *"I'm sending two of my guys to patrol your house and to stay with you for the evening. We'll try again tomorrow."*

"Okay," — I pulled on the wire strapped to my stomach, — "can I take this thing off?"

"Yes, I'll be there now to remove it."

I cleaned the mustard mess I'd made and placed the empty plate in the sink when someone knocked at the back door. I saw Piet's bald head before I saw his face.

"Hey," I said, opening the door. "Here," — I handed him the listening device he'd taped to my chest. I needed the bathroom and didn't want them listening to that. "Don't go anywhere." I dashed to the bathroom to relieve myself.

When I entered the kitchen again, Piet was nowhere in sight. "Where's Piet?" I asked the officer standing in the kitchen like a scary soldier.

"They needed him at another crime scene. He says he'll be back." The officer stepped closer to the back door with one hand on his weapon and glanced out of the window before turning back to me. "I'm Loyiso, part of Piet's Special Task Force." His serious tone stopped me in my tracks. He didn't wear the usual navy police uniform, but black tactical pants and a black shirt with a bulletproof vest.

"I'm Ophelia," I said and opened the fridge. "Is it just you hanging out with me tonight?"

"No," Loyiso said, staring out of the window again. "My colleague is in the front part of your house. You won't know he's here unless he wants you to see him." Loyiso glared at me with an intensity I'd never experienced before and became very nervous.

Not only was Loyiso large and muscular, but scary looking. He had a pistol across his chest that was easy to reach with his right hand, a sheathed knife behind his back, and another weapon strapped to his right thigh. He also had a scar on his cheek and another across his chin. I was sure Loyiso's massive hands could easily snap someone's neck, and the weapons were just for show.

"Have you handled guns before?"

"Once or twice," I said. My eyes flitted from his handgun to his hands, then up to his dark eyes.

Loyiso removed the handgun strapped to his chest and showed it to me. "It's a 9mm Sig Sauer," — he cocked the gun but kept the safety on, — "but this one," — Loyiso returned the Sig Sauer to his chest and reached for the rifle at his thigh, — "the automatic R4 packs a mean punch."

"I'll bet. Have you killed anyone with it?"

"What do you think?" he said, his expression emotionless.

"That it would be a firm, *yes*." I busied myself with a pan and switched on the stove. I wasn't hungry, but I didn't want to sit around and become a blubbering mess filled with nerves and anxiety; especially with a trained killer standing next to me.

"We've all killed. They were mostly bad," Loyiso said. His dark gaze was unnerving. "But we do our best to protect the innocent." He crossed the kitchen floor and before he left, he glanced over his shoulder and said, "Stay here while I check the rest of the house."

I opened my mouth, but nothing came out. Loyiso didn't wait for my response and disappeared into my dark house. He was intense, and I was happy to be left alone.

I added butter to the pan, cracked a couple of eggs inside, and scrambled the eggs while they cooked. Once the eggs were ready, I scooped them into a place and sat at the dining table. I had a bite, then moved the egg around on my plate.

I heard noises from somewhere in my house. When a dark shadow darted from the bathroom to my bedroom, I thought nothing of it. Loyiso was doing his job.

I still hadn't seen the other guy, but from what Loyiso had said, I may never see him. When footsteps sounded outside the lounge window, I brushed it off. Maybe it was the other guy.

I ate my dinner slowly and read messages from Jewel and Tony. I had to reschedule my coffee date with Tony to next week; there was too much happening and didn't want to involve him. But he was overly eager to meet with me.

A loud crash outside made me flinch, and I dropped my fork on my plate. The dark shadow of a man bolted out of my room with his weapon aimed. Loyiso held a finger to his lips and mouthed the word *'stay'* before heading towards the kitchen door.

Loyiso switched on the outside light and carefully opened the back door.

I stood up.

"Mitch?" Loyiso said. "Is that you or a stray cat?" He descended the stairs, closing the door behind him.

I peered over the kitchen counter but couldn't see anything. The backyard lights didn't reach all the dark corners, and I regretted not listening to the contractor who installed them.

The front door slammed closed, and I jumped. The lounge light blinked off. I felt like a sitting duck and glanced nervously around the kitchen. I didn't have the

138

chance to see who was in my house and hoped they didn't see me.

Someone had entered my home without announcing themselves, and I doubted it was the other guy who worked with Loyiso.

Whoever had arrived had spooked Loyiso who now left me alone. While I stood in the middle of my kitchen all I thought about was Jewel and not seeing her again. I didn't like any of these thoughts and pushed them away.

I sucked in a breath, reached for the kitchen light near the back door and switched it off. I grabbed the knife from the chopping board and headed for the walk-in pantry; it was large enough to hide in.

I clutched the knife handle until my fingers pained. My breath came in short, shallow bursts, and sweat peppered my forehead. I pressed the flat side of the knife against my forehead; the coolness brought a calmness I'd never known before and it scared me.

"O!" Piet yelled, followed by loud stomping across the kitchen floor. "It's Piet. O! Where are you?"

I exhaled a shaky breath and wiped a tear off my cheek. "Here," I said, slowly opening the pantry door. "I'm here Piet. You gave me a heart attack."

Piet darted around the corner and entered the kitchen with his pistol in his hand and wide eyes.

"Are you okay?" he asked.

"Yes, why?"

Piet exhaled audibly. "He was here."

"When? Loyiso just went outside when he heard a noise." I thumbed behind me.

"Where's Mitch?"

"I don't know. I don't even know what he looks like."

Piet frowned. "He was here when I left." He grabbed

his radio and asked Mitch to provide for his whereabouts. But when all he heard was static, Piet repeated his request. When he heard nothing from Mitch after five minutes, he spoke to someone on his cellphone and in hushed tones.

When Loyiso burst through the back door I almost dropped the knife. Piet aimed his weapon at Loyiso and swore under his breath when he realized it was only someone from his team. He lowered the pistol, as did Loyiso.

"Where's Mitch?"

"I haven't seen him," Loyiso said, crossing the kitchen floor. "It's not like him to ignore our calls." He pulled out his cellphone and dialed a number. "Nothing."

"I don't like this," Piet followed Loyiso into the dark lounge. "Why is your light out?" He asked, flicking the switch on and off, but nothing happened.

My frown deepened. "I don't know. It went off moments before you arrived."

"Grab the light from my vehicle, please, Loyiso."

Loyiso did as asked and returned with the flashlight, illuminating my couch. I followed the men but saw nothing; their large bodies blocked my view.

"What is it?" I asked, crouching to see better. I stopped moving when I saw thick red liquid on the tiles.

Chapter Thirty-Two

PIET USHERED me outside and called his team back to process the scene. I called Jacob who rode the twenty minutes to my place on his bicycle and waited outside with me.

"Are you okay?" Jacob asked, opening his cool drink. "Here," he said, handing me one.

"Thanks." I opened the bottle, my hands shaking, and enjoyed a sip. The cool, sweet, liquid went down my throat and I felt okay considering what had just happened. "I'll be okay. It's been a bit too much, you know."

"Uh-huh," — he sipped on his drink and closed it, — "do they know what happened?"

I rubbed the bridge of my nose and then my forehead.

"They think the killer gained access to my house and surprised Mitch." I wiped the tear with the back of my hand and sat on the damp grass.

Jacob sat beside me with his legs stretched out in front of him, placed his cold drink between his legs, and leaned back on his arms.

"Mitch died because of me—"

"Miss Ophelia, that's not right. This is not your fault. It's his," — he jerked his chin in the house's direction, — "the killer did this. Not you."

"I know but I still feel bad."

"Feel bad, but don't blame yourself."

We fell silent for a moment and I almost enjoyed being outside; until I remembered why I was sitting outside on the grass.

"Are we cleaning when they're done?"

"Yeah, we have to. I'm not paying another company to clean my house."

"I can do it."

I glanced at him. "Thanks for the offer, but I'll help."

"You don't want Thomas here?"

"No, I don't know if we can trust him."

Jacob nodded curtly. "I can keep an eye on him."

"Please, but do it in a way he won't notice. I don't want you getting hurt. If he does something wrong, I'll discipline him and give him a warning. If it happens again, only then can I fire him. I need to keep things above the law."

"Yes, Miss Ophelia."

We sat in silence and watched the police officers through the window process my lounge; there went another room marked by the killer and now the police. If I had the money, I'd tear down my house; but it was a lovely house. I loved it. I didn't want another house. But I didn't know if I could sleep in this house anymore.

It felt as though my life was in turmoil because of one person. This was not fair and I hated sounding like the victim. The things this killer had destroyed inside my home were just that, things. It's people's lives he destroyed that got to me the most.

But right now what mattered most was keeping my family safe and ensuring nobody else got hurt. It was the job of the police to protect citizens and they received a salary to put their lives in danger; they chose this profession. It wasn't up to me to protect them but the other way around.

I sighed wearily.

I needed to get a grip and stop feeling sorry for myself. I was still alive, a little shaky and scared, but alive.

Chapter Thirty-Three

THE MAN TOOK his bloodied shirt and pants off, threw them in the trashcan, and climbed into the shower. He combed his fingers through his blood-caked hair and moved under the cold water sprayer. He adjusted the hot tap until the water was the right temperature and continued washing his hair and body.

Once cleaned, the man climbed out of the shower and wrapped a towel around his waist, not bothering to dry his body first.

He exited the bathroom and paced from his living room, then back to his room, up and down until his skin felt dry enough to put his underwear on.

The man hung up his towel, thumbed the elastic band of his underwear, ignoring the suit laid out on his bed, and headed for his computer.

He side-eyed the mug of cold coffee and wished he'd made a fresh pot. He exhaled frustratingly and entered his password.

The browser opened, revealing live footage of the residence he'd been surveying for the last two weeks. There was nothing exciting happening other than police officers in various suits collecting evidence, again.

He smiled. Ophelia moved in front of the camera with her colleague, Jacob. They were speaking. The man wished he had bought a better camera with a speaker so he could listen in.

Ophelia had dark bags under her eyes, hadn't brushed her hair in a while, and she still wore yesterday's clothing.

The detective approached them, nodded, and thumbed over his shoulder.

Ophelia spoke and squeezed Jacob's shoulder, leaving the detective alone to speak with one of his officers.

Ophelia and Jacob entered her house.

"What are you doing?" The man said, engrossed with the footage. "You were so close, I could almost taste you. But that guy…"

The man scowled. He'd been so close to her last night that if he had reached out, he would've touched her. If it wasn't for that brute who had tried to stop him, and that other officer circling the house, he would've had Ophelia. She would've been here with him. He wouldn't dump her like the others. No, he wanted to take his time with her. He would take all the time in the world.

He clicked on another secure browser and various images popped up one at a time, showing his favorite first; his first kill.

The position of the woman was unnatural; she was on her side with her head tilted backwards, one arm stretched out behind her while the other under her head. She looked like she was running; he'd positioned her legs in such a way that if one glanced at the photo quickly, one assumed she was jumping over the stone near her left foot.

Beside her body was the necklace. The original necklace was used as a gift to the chosen woman. Then, as they admired their new jewelry, he'd hit them over their head, rendering them unconscious.

But what he wanted to do with Ophelia would take time. Lots of precious moments with her. He wanted to admire her beauty from afar while she struggled in her restraints, and then he'd destroy everything about her that made him want her.

Chapter Thirty-Four

JACOB METICULOUSLY CLEANED the lounge floor, taking care as if he were cleaning his own place.

We'd cleaned non-stop the last couple of hours and I'd asked him to go over it one last time while I submitted the forms for authorization to my insurance company. I didn't charge my insurance for the cleaning but for the furniture that needed to be destroyed; my favorite coffee table and both couches.

I glanced at the clean floor, at the spot where Mitch's body was, and shuddered at the thought of all the blood.

The killer had stabbed Mitch eleven times within a matter of seconds. Piet had mentioned that it was the last slash to Mitch's neck that had caused the most damage. If Piet hadn't arrived when he did, I may not have been around right now.

I was grateful that Mitch had two insurance policies that would pay out to his family upon his death; apparently the gorier the better. At least they would take care of his family, but still, it wasn't under great circumstances and I still felt awful about what had happened.

My insurance company replied saying they would get back to me with a decision and I pocketed my cellphone.

I pulled on fresh gloves and my respirator and entered my lounge finding Jacob cutting out the soiled pieces of the couch and about to dismantle the coffee table. It would be easier for us to load the pieces onto the back of the Ford instead of leaving them assembled.

We used a nearby company that handled all our biohazard waste; it was costly but worth it. Nobody should use items ruined by blood.

I helped Jacob dismantle the coffee table and carried the pieces to my truck. Once we loaded the furniture, we climbed out of our suits.

"Are you going to be okay here?" Jacob asked with concern in his tone.

I smiled, but it didn't reach my eyes. "I should be okay," I said, folding my suit and placing it on the couch in my office. "Do you feel like driving with me to get rid of the stuff?"

"Sure," he said, placing his suit beside mine. "I have nothing else planned this afternoon."

"You don't need to sleep?" We'd been awake since last night, waiting for the police to finish what they were doing before we could clean.

"No, all that coffee has kept me awake. Besides, you can't go alone."

A police officer entered the room talking to someone on his cellphone. "Miss Blaine," he said, pocketing his cellphone. "We're done for the moment. Are you going anywhere soon?"

"We need to take the couches and coffee table to be

destroyed. Then I want to go relieve some stress at Thys's gym."

"We'll escort you," the police officer said, calling another plain-clothed officer over. "Marcel will shadow you and drive your vehicle—"

I raised my hand to stop him. "I don't need anyone driving me around."

"It's for your safety, Miss Blaine. Should the killer approach you while driving, we won't have control over the situation." He left his words hanging, and I hated I couldn't do anything about it.

I groaned inwardly, my shoulders sagging. "Fine, but Jacob is joining us."

"That's fine," Marcel said. His tone was hoarse, reminding me of a chain smoker. He glanced Jacob up and down, his left eyebrow raised slightly. "He can sit in the back. Where do you need to go?"

"There's a medical waste disposal in Blackheath we can use."

Marcel's eyebrow arched higher. "That's quite a distance. Do you drive out there often?"

"Only when we need to, and it has to be done today."

He nodded, but I could tell he was unhappy about it.

"Let's go before we hit traffic." Marcel turned around, but before he left, he glanced over his shoulder, adding, "Where are your keys?"

"By the front door."

Marcel and the other police officer left Jacob and me alone. After a moment of silence, I leaned closer to Jacob. "That man is intense. Are you sure you're happy to hang out with me?"

"Yes, Miss Ophelia," Jacob said, his eyes twinkling with

humor. "Everything will be ok." He patted my shoulder and went to the bathroom.

————

WE DROPPED the items at the waste disposal, paid the fee, and I directed Marcel where to drive. He'd never heard of Thys's gym; which was in the middle of Somerset's industrial area.

Marcel parked the car and followed us inside. I doubted the killer would come anywhere near me while I was here, but I'd remain vigilant anyway even with my bodyguard.

I greeted Thys who stood near his office door watching Marcel with hawk eyes. I entered the bathroom to change and when I came back out Marcel and Jacob were playing on the gym equipment. They tried to pick up the heaviest weight, laughing when they realized they couldn't lift it.

Jacob glanced my way as if sensing my stare. Marcel stopped what he was doing and stood like a soldier.

I flinched when someone grabbed my shoulder, spun around, and slammed my fists into his chest. Thys doubled over, wheezing.

"Shit, I'm sorry," I said, rubbing his back. "You gave me a fright."

"Ah," Thys said, coughing. After a moment, he finally stood straight, his face blood red. "At least you could defend yourself on instinct," he said, smiling.

I grinned, remembering the last time someone grabbed my shoulder. I had done nothing to stop Eric. That I'd felt paralyzed when he touched me. At least now my head was back in the present.

"Are you okay?" I asked, rubbing his back.

"I will be." Thys stretched his back and rubbed his sternum. "Is everything okay?" He jerked his chin in Marcel's direction.

"No, but it will be. All I want to do is beat someone up."

"Hmm, maybe I should pair you up with someone else." He chuckled. "But someone who can handle your punches because I don't think I can breathe properly yet."

"Now I feel bad—"

He chuckled again. "Don't worry about it," — he was about to touch my shoulder but thought otherwise, — "maybe I shouldn't touch you again. That seems to be a trigger."

When I opened my mouth to apologize again, he raised his hand to shush me.

"It's all good, Ophelia. I know you won't hurt someone on purpose. I really am impressed by how you handled yourself. You've got good instincts."

I beamed. "Thank you. Maybe I should take my frustrations out on the bag instead." I glanced at Marcel who was punching the other bag.

"Good idea. I don't think I have enough emergency supplies to take care of everyone you beat up." Thys grabbed gloves. "Come, let's set you up."

Thys first strapped my wrists and knuckles, then helped me pull on the gloves. I readied my stance and started punching the bag with all my weight behind each hit until I was sweaty, exhausted, and hungry.

I ignored the stares from others, removed the gloves and unwrapped the tape from my hands. My hands hurt and my arms pained, but it felt great. It felt as though I'd done something constructive instead of sitting around like a victim.

I entered the bathroom and showered quickly. Once

dressed, I packed my things and joined the men. Jacob and Marcel were chatting to Thys near the equipment.

I didn't feel like small talk, or any kind of talk, and waited by the exit. The cool air from outside was pleasant against my still warm skin; my arms pebbling from the sensation.

It felt good to still be alive, and that I'd be in Jewel's life for a few more years. But I knew I couldn't get too excited. We still had a killer to catch.

When someone with a hoody and shorts brushed past me as they entered the gym, he barely gave me a second glance and went straight to Thys; he looked like the same guy who met with Thys after our dinner date a couple of days ago.

Thys followed the man, who glanced around nervously. He whispered something to Thys. They shook hands, and then he walked out of the gym.

Thys pocketed something. When he glanced up and saw me staring, he smiled guiltily.

I approached. "Can I ask what that was, or will you lie to me?" I said, closing the gap, ensuring Marcel didn't hear. If that's a drug deal I'd just witnessed, I didn't want Thys getting into trouble... yet. I wanted to understand what was happening first.

Thys pulled the item out of his pocket and opened his hand. "It's for my grandmother." He turned the packet over so that I could read the label.

"What's wrong with your grandmother?"

"She has cancer and is in a frail care center. This," — he pinched the corner of the bag and held it up, — "helps her nausea and to sleep. It's the only thing she smokes. She also has the oil, which she drops onto a piece of cake or tart or whatever dessert she's eating. It helps with the pain."

"Sorry, I can only imagine what she's going through. You should mention to your dealer that perhaps he shouldn't wear a hoody. It makes the exchange look suspicious." I smiled warmly.

"He's embarrassed about the bald spot on his head. Ever since I've known him, he wears a hoody," Thys said, heading for his office. "Let me put this down and I'll walk you out."

These days, one could buy CBD oils over the counter at any health shop or pharmacy; it was now legal to use cannabis. I'd heard it did wonders for anxiety, cancer, and even joint ache. The list went on. If the pharmaceutical company couldn't help with something, why not use nature? At least Thys's grandmother was relatively pain-free.

Thys ran back to me and gave me a hug. "I hope your day gets better. I know you've been going through a rough patch lately and I can see it's been hard on you. Know that I'm here whenever you need me."

"Thank you, Thys. I appreciate that," I said, hugging him back. He smelled like aftershave and sweat, but it was pleasant. His muscles moved beneath my touch, and it was then I realized how strong he was. He didn't brag about what he could do, but I knew he held back whenever he and I sparred together.

I was so suspicious of everyone with what was happening. But it relieved me to know that Thys was one of the good guys. He had been nothing but supportive, and that mishap of his dealer was nothing more than Thys taking care of his grandmother.

"The gym will be closed for the next couple of days," Thys said, bringing me out of my thoughts. "I'm bringing in some guys to repaint the walls and replace the mats." He pointed at the torn mat we stood on. "After a good couple of years, it's time for a replacement."

"Okay, good luck. I'm sure it will look great." I glanced at Marcel, who was by the door with Jacob to one side. "I need to go," — I leaned closer to Thys and pressed my palm against his chest, — "before I get into trouble."

Thys chuckled, and it sounded good. "I see. Good luck and call me if you need anything. I'll help however I can."

I stared at Thys for longer than necessary and my smile reached my eyes. "Thanks, I appreciate that. Hopefully, I won't need to. It's nice to know that you will be there."

I squeezed Thys's shoulder and left him standing near his office. I just reached Jacob and Marcel when something whizzed past me, followed by blood spattering all over my face and chest.

Chapter Thirty-Five

THE MAN WOULDN'T HESITATE AGAIN. When the large, plain-clothed police officer went down, he charged at Ophelia. Her colleague reached for him but the man smashed his fist into his face, rocking his head backwards and he crashed to the floor.

The gym owner had stumbled, jumped to his feet when he saw what was happening and closed the gap. The man fired his weapon again. Ophelia ducked, and the bullet struck the gym owner in his hip, sending him to the floor.

The other patrons scattered in search of a hiding spot, but the man didn't care about them. He was only here for her.

The man grabbed Ophelia, pulling her up by her arm. She yelped in pain, trying to hit his arm off of her, but he held onto her like a vice grip.

With Ophelia in his grasp, the man half-dragged, and half-carried her to his vehicle. Ophelia continued fighting him off, but he couldn't allow her to get away this time. He needed to subdue her if he wanted to leave the parking area.

There were people in the parking lot but they climbed into their cars, avoiding the scene before them. It relieved him that they minded their own business. He didn't feel like shooting anyone else.

"No!" Ophelia yelled as he opened the car door, pushing her into the seat.

"Keep still," the man groaned.

Ophelia kicked him in the groin area, making him furious. He didn't hesitate this time and hit her in the face. She was momentarily stunned, and blinked up at him before trying to push him away.

The man smacked his fist into her cheek, rendering her unconscious.

Chapter Thirty-Six

MY HEAD THUMPED LOUDLY, and my left cheek and eye were swollen. I stretched and swallowed hard, wishing for water or a large glass of wine and a painkiller.

"Good evening," he said. His voice echoed in the small bedroom. I opened my eyes but he was a blur to my left in my peripheral vision.

I glanced up at the ceiling; it was no longer white, but a light shade of yellow. Perhaps a smoker had lived in this room. The bedding smelled fresh, but the stench of old smoke and soup wafted in the air.

I tried sitting up, but my head ached too much. It relieved me he hadn't tied me down or handcuffed me to a bedpost. Not wanting to be an easier target than I already was, I forced myself to sit up with my back against the icy wall.

"Why, Eric?" I said, carefully rubbing the sleep from my eyes. "Why kill all those women? Why come after me?" I sighed wearily. I turned to look at him and my breath caught in my throat. He was no longer as well-groomed as before. His dark, unwashed hair was oily and on his face. His hands and fingernails were dirty. The t-shirt wasn't ironed and his torn shorts hadn't seen the inside of a washing machine in ages.

Nothing about Eric screamed sophistication like it did the first time I met him. Even when we hiked together, he seemed put together; unlike now.

The muscles in my back spasmed from sitting at an odd angle, but I wouldn't show that I was in pain. I wanted nothing from him.

"Why do people always want to know '*why*' someone does anything?" he said, standing up and pacing at the foot of the bed. "Psychiatrists are so excited to dissect the villain in the story that nobody questions the *victim*. People think they're innocent. But they aren't."

"So the victim is to blame in your story?" I asked, masking my disgust.

Eric laughed maniacally and stopped pacing. He stood at the foot of the bed, laughing like it was the funniest thing I'd said.

"Ophelia, you are funny." He traversed around the bed and sat down again. His dark eyes were a stern warning; he was unstable. "Nobody helped my father when she emptied his bank account." He spat out the words with so much hate, I could read it on his face. "Nobody helped my father when she left her only son home alone while she went out on a *date*."

I flinched when Eric jumped to his feet and started pacing again.

"Nobody helped my father when he came home to her empty closet and a crying toddler. Nobody helped when we were starving. Nobody helped when she returned to leave a newborn baby behind. A baby that was not my father's, yet he took it upon himself to care for it. We were the victims in her story. Why did nobody care about us?"

Eric stopped pacing and stared intensely. It looked as if there was more he wanted to share. I opened my mouth to say something when he continued speaking.

"My uncle was not a nice man," he said, opening his palm and rubbing the finger with the scar. "He enjoyed teaching me valuable lessons."

It made sense. Eric, his father, and half-brother were victims. What they had endured was terrible. The things his uncle must've done to him were awful, too, but...

"Eric, I'm not trying to make what you and your father went through sound like it meant nothing. But you hurt women who didn't deserve your wrath—"

"They did!" He yelled, making me flinch. "They all start off sweet and innocent, batting their eyelashes and blushing. But then I got to know them, and as they revealed their true selves, I discovered they were sluts, easy, and slept with anyone for five minutes of attention or worse, money. They were all like *her*," he said the last sentence through gritted teeth.

"Like your mother?" I asked, trying not to provoke him, but failing. I glanced at the open door, hoping it would be an easy escape.

"Yes, they were *all* like that woman who gave birth to me."

I moved slightly, scooting farther away from him while still on the bed. My eyes caught sight of the bedside tables, but there was nothing on them I could use to defend myself with; unless I grabbed the lamp, but the cord could be secured in place.

"Why me?" I asked, turning my attention to him once more. "I did nothing to you."

"You almost went on a date with Tony."

I swallowed hard. He knew about Tony. "That was you?" He had sounded so different online than in person; like he had a completely different personality.

"What do you think?" His grin split his face in two. "*I'd love to meet you. How soon?*" He said mockingly.

I groaned inwardly and thanked my lucky stars I didn't meet with him when he wanted to... I knew there was a reason he was so pushy but I couldn't; it wasn't the right time, and I had so much going on.

"Did you know Lucy was my best friend?"

"Not at first." His tone was no longer filled with rage. "When she mentioned she worked for a crime scene cleaning company, I put two and two together." His smile returned, making me uncomfortable. "It made the experience fun and long-lasting."

I groaned inwardly. It physically pained me thinking of all the things Lucy went through at his hands. I had to get away from him before it was too late. My eyes darted to the open door, and I scooted closer to the edge of the bed.

"I was there that first day." He continued.

That caught my attention, and I stared at him. "What do you mean?"

"The first crime scene. The woman with the greenhouse in her backyard."

The lines between my brows deepened. "The one with the dead dog and necklace on the floor?"

He nodded. "I watched you pick up the necklace, and I laughed at your facial expression when you saw the dog. It's not my best work, but it had to be done. She was another one who lied. She said she didn't have a dog, and couldn't wait to get me in her bed." He chortled.

Bile rose in my throat, and I swallowed hard, shuddering at the taste. There was so much wrong with this guy. He'd need a team of medical help. He had killed the dog gruesomely and it pained me to see the aftermath. Although I hadn't seen the woman's body, I remembered all the blood left behind. Eric was not well.

"Is that when you decided to pursue me?"

"Yes, I'd never seen someone work as meticulously as you did that day. I watched you for a while." He smiled kindly as he stared at me. It was unnerving. "You're the first woman I want to get to know. You are special to me, Ophelia."

I tried not to show my disgust, but my expression angered Eric; he fisted the chair arm and stood up.

"This is not the way it's supposed to go." He yelled. "You were supposed to tell me you admire my work."

I didn't want to anger him any more than I already had, and thought it best to keep quiet.

"You were supposed to tell me you'll join me." He snorted, spat out whatever was in his mouth, and paced.

I dropped my right leg onto the floor while carefully keeping an eye on Eric as he paced and mumbled to himself. He fisted his hair, let go, and then placed his hands on his hips, muttering under his breath.

Slowly, I moved off of the bed and placed both feet on the carpet. There was something squishy beneath my feet and between my toes, but I didn't want to divert my attention from Eric and look to see what it was.

Carefully, I placed all my weight onto my feet as I stood up; the cold squishy stuff oozed between my toes. I gagged and quickly corrected myself.

I stepped closer to the door.

Eric continued pacing, oblivious to what I was doing, but I continued keeping a watchful eye as I moved closer to the door, the squishy stuff between my toes becoming less.

When I reached the door, Eric stopped pacing. He glanced at the bed, then around the room. His eyes found mine. My heart thundered in my chest, and a cool layer of sweat covered my skin.

If I darted out of the room, he would follow. I didn't know the layout of the house and was unsure of the way out. But my instincts told me to run. I would take my chances jumping out of a nearby window if it didn't have burglar bars on.

I flinched.

Eric lunged for me.

I bolted through the doorway and ran down the stairs; I ran so fast I couldn't stop myself in time and smashed into the wall at the bottom; my left hip and shoulder pained but I ignored it.

The front door was to the right. I reached for it. Locked. I swore under my breath and headed down the long corridor towards another open room; the kitchen. The back door was open, and I pushed through the screen door, into an enclosure with tinted black windows.

"No!" I yelled, slamming my fists onto the solid windows.

Footsteps echoed in the room. Eric was closing the distance.

Chapter Thirty-Seven

ERIC STALKED HIS PREY. She had cornered herself in his enclosure, made specifically for her. He couldn't help but smile.

The whimpering woman was all talk and nothing else. Although he'd seen her defend herself at the gym, he doubted she could defend herself against him. If she behaved as she did in the coffee shop last week, she would freeze. He counted on her freezing.

He entered the newly enclosed room. Ophelia stood to one side, her body shaking and her eyes wide. A grin split his face in two. He loved it when the women were afraid; shaking like a leaf. The fear of the unknown. He counted on them being afraid of him; of what he'd do to them. He thrived on it.

He also knew what his expression looked like; dark, moody, and dangerous. He'd practiced perfecting that look in the mirror exactly for this, so he could enjoy the look on their faces—on Ophelia's face.

It wasn't only their frightened expression, but the smell

of fear that lingered in the air. Some of them urinated, and others sweated. Everything about the situation left him happy.

Eric had options for Ophelia. He didn't want it over quickly like the others. No. He wanted to take his time with her. He wanted her to feel everything he would do to her body while he savored the smells and sounds that came from her.

While Eric daydreamed of the possibilities. He didn't see Ophelia's approach. He didn't see the object in her hand. Nor did he feel the object pierce his stomach like a hot knife through butter. The screwdriver he'd left behind while renovating the room.

Eric screamed, swatting her hand away from him.

"Take that, asshole." Ophelia slammed her fist into his throat, stopping his breathing. When Eric doubled over she brought her elbows down onto his back, cracking ribs.

She pushed him away from her and he crashed to the ground, leaving him to suffocate on the breath in his throat and to nurse the gushing wound.

Ophelia ran back inside the house.

Chapter Thirty-Eight

I WON'T CRY, I won't cry, I won't cry. I said my mantra as I tried the front door again and the lounge windows. He'd locked everything tightly. The only way out was back up the stairs and out a window, but only if the windows had no burglar bars.

I climbed the stairs and entered the room he'd held me in earlier and froze in the doorjamb. Only then did I realize what I had stood in. The squishy liquid in the once white furry carpet was coagulating blood. I took a moment and stared at my red stained feet and cringed.

I entered the room carefully, half expecting Eric to jump out from under the bed, but I knew he was downstairs. That didn't stop my imagination from running wild with me. I found the source of the blood and could go no farther.

He had placed the naked woman in an unnatural position in the center of the room at the foot of the bed. He had sliced her skin carefully and peeled it back in a pattern that reminded me of blossoming roses. Beside the victim was a necklace similar to the one I'd found in the greenhouse.

I whimpered into my hands, tears streaming down my cheeks.

She wasn't breathing, and I didn't want to touch her; there could be evidence Eric left behind. I walked past her corpse and headed for the window. I sighed with relief; there were no bars on the windows.

I groaned as the window creaked open and smiled as I sucked in a deep breath of fresh air, shedding tears of happiness. I glanced over my shoulder and I was still alone. Slowly, I climbed onto the ledge and dangled my legs over before dropping onto the roof beneath me.

Sounds of footsteps up the stairs forced me to move quickly and, without thinking, jumped into the flower bed below.

Chapter Thirty-Nine

I LANDED with a solid oomf sound, knocking the air out of my lungs; the impact from landing stung my feet, shins, and hands. I struggled to climb to my feet; my left ankle pained.

"Get back here!" Eric yelled from the open window. He carefully climbed out, clutching the wound at his side. Blood poured between his fingers and it made me glad to see him suffer.

I glanced around for a way out and limped towards the winding driveway.

"Shit," Eric mumbled behind me. When I glanced over my shoulder, he climbed back through the window and disappeared inside the house.

I hobbled down the long, winding driveway, glancing at both sides of the single road; across the vast land stood tall trees and thick bushes in the distance. I didn't realize Eric was this wealthy unless he had rented this place as well, or the house belonged to the deceased woman in the room.

I didn't want to turn around when the front door

slammed shut. I was half-walking, half-limping at a brisk pace and needed to continue forward and to safety.

I headed for the trees on my left after the sound of a vehicle started. The bushes were thicker on this side, and I hoped I could find a hiding spot while escaping him.

The car zoomed past me. The brakes squeaked, and he reversed.

I continued hobbling through the tall grass and thick bushes. I headed for a copse of trees. The vehicle moved in the opposite direction from me and I relaxed but not for long, I needed to get out of there.

Thorn branches scratched my left shoulder and leg. My chest ached as air burned my lungs. I pushed branches out of my face and continued forward.

The pain in my ankle worsened, but I couldn't stop now. I continued pushing my hands through thick branches and leaves until they struck something solid; a tall hedge.

I felt the hedge to find a way through or over. I walked along the side of the tall hedge, but the greenery was thick and overgrown.

I dusted spiderwebs out of my face, thinking that under normal circumstances, I would've enjoyed the scenery; I would welcome the smell of dirt and wet leaves while having a picnic and watching others play games. But running away from a killer wasn't the type of sport I enjoyed. It usually ended with one of us dead.

I heard nothing apart from my breathing and leaves scraping against branches when twigs snapped behind me. I froze, glanced around, and waited. More twigs snapped in the distance. His footsteps were getting closer.

I glanced around and squinted in the distance. There was a dark patch in the hedge that might be a way out. I limped in that direction, careful not to make a noise. When

I no longer heard him behind me, I crouched and went onto my hands and knees; relieving my aching ankle.

I almost cried out in joy when I found a hole in the hedge; it was big enough for me to squeeze through. After checking for spiders, I entered the hole.

I'd just squeezed my shoulders through the hole when someone grabbed my good ankle. I yelped and kicked with my left foot, crying out in pain when my injured ankle hit a root that stuck out of the ground.

"Where do you think you're going?" Eric grunted behind me, tightening his grip on my ankle.

Before he could grab my other foot, I had to get away from him. I doubted he could climb through the tight hole and I could have a head start.

"Get away from me, you psycho," I said through gritted teeth and gripped the thick roots to pull myself closer to freedom.

When Eric neared and reached for my other foot, I kicked. The bones in my ankle crunched on impact. I cried out in pain, and he let go of my other ankle to nurse his bleeding nose.

I fell into a ditch after pulling myself through in one swift motion. My left ankle had doubled in size, with a dark bruise covering the outside. It relieved me to be out, but now I needed to get to safety.

"Get back here, you bitch!" He yelled as he tried climbing through the small hole. "I'm going to get you," he said sinisterly. The tone of his voice made my skin crawl.

I crawled farther away from the hole and out of the ditch. I shed tears when my hands touched the road. Unsure of which direction to go, I continued crawling to my left.

Eric threw sticks and branches over the hedge; reminding me of a baby throwing their toys out of the cot.

My knees ached as I crawled over stones and broken pieces of glass, but I didn't care or feel that pain. The only thought I had was needing to flee.

When a car approached, I raised my hands in the air so they would see me and waved frantically. The car slowed, its tinted windows revealed nothing of who was inside.

I looked over my shoulder and didn't see signs that Eric was still there. I didn't see the car he was driving earlier and this could be him. I lowered my hands.

The car rolled to a stop, and the tinted driver's window came down. "Everything okay?" the man said with kind green eyes.

"Please help me."

Chapter Forty

ERIC COULDN'T ALLOW Ophelia to get away. He would kill anybody who came between them and he had his sights on the driver who had stopped to help her.

He pressed the tape harder against his side to stop the bleeding. He no longer felt any pain as the adrenaline he'd injected into his thigh coursed through his veins.

Eric grunted and lunged for the driver with a knife.

"Behind you!" Ophelia screamed as the man helped her into the car.

The driver spun around as Eric grabbed him, driving the blade deep into his sternum and twisting up. The driver clutched Eric's shoulders. His green eyes darkened. His grip relaxed and his arms fell limply to his sides.

Eric pushed the knife deeper, and the driver coughed up blood. Eric removed the knife and let him go. He crashed to the ground. His eyes stared vacantly at Eric's feet.

Eric's eyes flitted to the vehicle as Ophelia scooted over into the driver's side. She closed the door and smashed the gas.

He lunged for the open window and grabbed at her throat. She batted him away, but he grabbed her hand and pulled. She cried out in pain, desperately trying to push him away.

He unlocked the door with his left hand and opened it.

Ophelia corrected the steering wheel before the car crashed into the ditch. He grabbed the steering wheel and yanked hard. The vehicle veered to the right. He jumped into the car and continued pulling right.

Ophelia pushed against him as the car hit the ditch. Eric fell into the open door and onto the grass in the ditch. Ophelia closed the door and placed the car into reverse, but it didn't budge. The left back wheel and right front wheel were raised and unable to grip the road.

Ophelia swore under her breath and climbed out of the car on the other side.

Another car approached slowly.

Eric clambered out of the ditch and grabbed Ophelia before she could flag them down. He pressed the blade against her face and she dropped her arms.

"You aren't going anywhere," he said against her cheek.

Chapter Forty-One

I STOOD FROZEN as Eric moved his hand, trailing the knife down my neck and shoulder, before pressing it into my back.

The car slowed, and the driver let his window down. "Ophelia?" Thomas said, stopping his car. "What's going on here?" He glanced at Eric with a raised eyebrow.

I exhaled a relieved breath and tried not to whimper. I mouthed the word 'help', but Thomas was too busy scowling at Eric to notice me.

"Carry on driving," Eric said, stepping back with me. "This doesn't concern you." He snaked his left arm around my waist and kept his knife against my side, ensuring I didn't move.

Thomas glanced at my ankle, Eric's arm around my waist, and then at Eric's face. He cut the engine and climbed out of the car.

"Get back inside your car," Eric warned.

"I mean no harm," Thomas said, raising his hands. He

glanced at the vehicle in the ditch and the body on the road. "Who is that?" He jerked his chin in the corpse's direction.

"Now isn't the time," Eric said, moving us closer to Thomas's car.

"You know I'll never get in your way, brother," Thomas said, grinning. He combed his dirty fingers through his oily hair. "I wish you told me you wanted her *this* badly. Besides, you know I'm up for any action." He thrust his pelvis and licked his lips. "At least this one is pretty. And you know I always share."

My mind performed a somersault upon hearing that word... *Brother*. They were half-brothers.

"Now look what you've done. She's gone all silent," Eric chuckled. "You know I like them scared and vocal."

I closed my mouth and swallowed, blinking back the moisture in my eyes. "You kill together?"

Thomas roared with laughter. "Of course. Brothers who kill together, stay together. We do everything together, or take turns while the other goes to work."

Eric chuckled.

I stared, dumbfounded.

"She looks broken," Thomas said. "And you barely touched her." He glanced at my ankle again. "That must hurt."

"It's fine," I said, wishing for help.

Eric pressed his head against mine and sniffed my hair. I pulled away from him, but he tightened his hold on my arm.

"Why?" I asked. It was futile asking questions, but I needed to stall them because the moment both men had me where they wanted me, I'd be dead shortly thereafter. At least out in the open, somebody was bound to drive past. I hoped.

"When they separated us from our father, he went to his butcher uncle," — Thomas pointed at Eric, — "and I went to an old man who enjoyed hurting animals and stuffing them." Thomas smiled but there was pain behind his eyes. "You see, some kids' lives aren't as rosy as others," Thomas said, sounding angry.

"Now be fair," Eric said. "Our father got his life on track and claimed us once more. Unfortunately, by then, so much damage was done," Eric said sadly. "Those men are now gone." He smiled. "Enough of this bullshit," — he pulled on my arm, — "I don't enjoy sitting out here. A cop could drive by any moment."

Thomas chortled. "Cops hardly come here, man. Relax."

"Don't tell me to relax," Eric said in a stern voice. He yanked on my arm and almost dragged me to Thomas's car. "Get in," he commanded, and I limped.

"Where are we going?" I asked nervously, glancing at the dirty seat, and begrudgingly climbed inside. I pushed old food wrappers and cans off the seat. Eric almost sat on my lap when he pushed in beside me.

"We need to get back inside," he thumbed the hedge. "Hurry," he yelled at Thomas, who was removing the wallet from the corpse.

"Chill, man. This guy's loaded," — he flashed notes and a shiny new cellphone, — "I struck gold."

"You're such an idiot. You're already loaded, yet you scrounge around like a homeless person." Eric rolled his eyes and squeezed my arm.

I yelped and yanked my arm out of his grasp. "You're hurting me."

"That ain't hurting. Wait, you'll feel what I can do, eventually."

Thomas put his car into first gear and pulled away slowly, turning left at the next road. The overgrown road went around the property and stopped at a large wrought-iron gate.

"Just once can I push it open with the car?"

Eric sighed frustratingly. "Sure," he said, looking at me and smiling. "This is exciting." Then he winced and his features turned darker, menacingly. "You're going to pay for this," — he pointed at his side, his clothing bloody and damp, — "it hurts."

The car inched forward and hit the gate with a soft tap. Thomas smashed the gas and the gate creaked open, hitting the sides of the fence and sped through before the gates bounced back and hit us.

"Yes!" Thomas said, laughing.

"You're such a child."

"Shut up."

I watched their exchange, reminding me of young boys fighting over a toy car. They were juvenile at best, and psychotic at worst. I didn't want to engage with either side; they were equally deadly.

I didn't know what they were going to do to me. I saw the woman upstairs and knew it was Eric's handy work. I assumed he would do something similar to me. Unfortunately, nobody knew I was here and I couldn't fight against both of them.

I was about to die and I thought of Jewel; I wanted to hug her, comb my fingers through her thick hair, and kiss her cheek one last time. I wanted to do so many things. My whole life was ahead of me; I couldn't die now.

My ankle throbbed, pulling me out of my self-pity.

The men continued their childish banter.

I watched the scenery as we drove through the large backyard. "Is this your house?" I asked no one in particular.

"Nah," Eric said. "I met the owner online; a lonely divorcee with money to burn. I first transferred the funds out of her account and into our offshore account before playing with her. Did you see my roses on her body?" Eric stared at me.

"I did, crafty handiwork." My tone came out sarcastic, and I didn't care. If they were going to kill me, I would give them all the trouble I could.

Thomas harrumphed. "You mean I was the one who met with her, posing as *Tony*. You know I hate the older ones. They're usually too independent and feisty."

"Quit complaining. You enjoyed her."

"Yeah, but still. The next old one is yours." He shuddered. "All those wrinkles."

They continued complaining while I paid attention to the lawnmower in the middle of nowhere; like someone had stopped cutting the grass and left. In the distance stood a shed with its door open. Movement caught my eye, and I flinched, closing my mouth. The man pressed his finger to his lips, pointed to the side, and headed in that direction.

My eyes filled with tears. The brothers hadn't seen the caretaker, but he'd seen them; he knew what was going on. I hoped he had called the police, and I hoped he would help me before they killed me.

Chapter Forty-Two

THOMAS PARKED the car inside the open garage and climbed out.

Eric stared at me. "You're really beautiful," he said, sounding sincere. If it wasn't for his killer hobby, he may have been a nice guy to date.

I glanced away.

We sat in silence for a moment, but I still felt his stare; like a weight against my left shoulder.

I turned to look at him. "You don't have to do this, Eric," I said his name to humanize him. I wasn't something he could just play with and discard. I was a person with feelings and I had a family I cared for. "Why don't you disappear with your brother? I won't say anything. Just leave."

"Haha hahaha, I wish, Ophelia. But I can't. You see, you're like the whale I've been searching for my whole adult life. I can't let you go. Not now, not ever." He opened the car door and climbed out. He stood outside with an outstretched hand as if we were on a date and wanted to help me out of the car.

If it wasn't for my ankle, I wouldn't need him to walk. I sighed, scooted to the edge of the seat and placed my good foot on the ground first and stood up, keeping my left ankle up. I reached for Eric's hand, but he didn't take it. He snaked his arm around my waist and half-carried me to the door that led through the kitchen and down a set of stairs.

Thomas waited in the kitchen with a knife in each hand. "Where are we doing this?"

"Not yet," Eric said, leading me to a room down the hallway. "You know I want to take my time with her."

"You're no fun," Thomas yelled, dropping the knives on the counter with a loud clunk. "You have an hour, then I'm coming in." He stomped in the opposite direction.

"You must excuse my brother. He doesn't have manners," Eric said, unlocking a door and pushing it open. "I'd like us to start here, then we'll make our way to the enclosure you were inside earlier. I'll ensure your death is enjoyable for both of us."

I ignored his words; they were not comforting. I glanced from Eric's face to the room he'd opened and froze. My mouth dropped open at the sterile sight.

A white table stood in the middle of the dark room. The table shone brightly in contrast to the darkness. Eric had mounted a light in the middle of the ceiling to highlight the white table. Then on either side of the white table hung various instruments on the wall; knives, hooks, and various size machetes. It was something out of a movie; *Hostel* came to mind. The difference was, in the movie, the victims were unaware of their outcome. I knew they would slaughter me. It would be slow and torturous based on the expression on Eric's face.

"I'll make sure you're comfortable," Eric said, disappearing into the room.

There was a minute head start. I could run out of the kitchen and garage, but not fast enough. I had a broken ankle and could barely lean on it. If I tried running away, Eric would reach me faster than I could say *'backwards'* and then he'd most likely be angry.

I flinched when Eric returned with a needle in his hands. I moved backwards, keeping my balance by leaning on the walls.

"Don't worry, you'll be awake and can see my work of art. You just won't feel anything."

"Please, Eric, don't do this."

"But I do, Ophelia. I have to do it all. I have to see what you're made of."

It was the perfect time for the caretaker to rescue me; to burst through the doors with a machine gun and blast Eric and Thomas away. But nobody came through the door. Nobody was here except us, and I didn't like the odds.

I felt the prick of the needle, then nothing; the clear liquid took hold of me almost instantaneously. My eyes widened as I fell.

Eric caught me before I crashed to the ground.

My painful ankle felt fine, but I couldn't move any limbs.

Eric picked me up, cradling me like a baby against his body, and carried me to the table. I hated having my face pressed against his shoulder. He smelled like cloves, eucalyptus, black pepper, and nutmeg. And underneath that scent was sweat. I tried pushing against him, but I barely moved.

He brought me to the white table, carefully laying me on top, and positioned my head on a small pillow. He dusted my hair off my chest and face, then kissed my forehead. I cringed inwardly, grateful I could still blink and close my eyes.

"You are beautiful on my table," he said, standing straight where I could easily see him. "It's as if I made it for you. You fit perfectly. Your skin is rosy and clean. And you smell," — he breathed air over his teeth and near my ear, — "exquisite for someone who has activated her fight-or-flight responses."

Eric moved away from me, trailing his fingertips over my collarbone, right breast, stomach, and then down my hip and thigh. He squeezed my calf muscle before opening the closet.

I shut my eyes tightly with each touch he laid against my body. He was vile and repulsed me.

The hinges squeaked open. He had packed one side of the closet with junk; like he stuffed everything there to make space for what he really wanted—a white sheet folded neatly on the middle shelf. He took the sheet, opened it up, and placed it over my feet.

Meticulously, Eric removed my shoes one at a time and placed them on the floor near his feet. He rubbed the good ankle, then when it was the left ankle's turn, he kissed the top of my foot.

"It's broken and you've probably torn muscles," he said, carefully turning my foot this way and that way without applying pressure. I was grateful I couldn't feel anything; the bones of that ankle crunched beneath his touch. Then he covered my feet. "There, we must keep the feet warm throughout the procedure."

The moment he said procedure, a whimper escaped my lips and tears streamed down the sides of my face and into my ears.

"Shh, it will be okay. You won't feel a thing."

"Please, Eric. Please don't do this. My daughter—"

"Will be taken care of. I'll make sure your lowlife ex

looks after her." He patted my thigh and pulled out scissors from behind his back. "This may be cold," he said, cutting the hem of my jeans. He sliced through my jeans easily and right to the top; the sharp blades barely struggling at the belt loops.

"Now for this side," he said cheerfully, moving around the table. As he walked around, he kept his free hand on me; his fingertips barely touching me. It's as if he wanted me to feel comfortable in my demise.

"Did the others feel anything?" I asked, swallowing another whimper.

Eric stopped on my left-hand side, his free hand on my thigh. "They felt something," he said gravely. "I didn't give them half of what I gave you. Sometimes I gave them nothing at all and they felt everything." He smiled, but his eyes were dead. I didn't think he had any compassion. "Now where was I?" He grabbed the hem of my left leg and sliced easily through the material.

Once he had cut the jeans into ribbons, his smile widened when he saw my underwear.

"You see. This is why you're special. You wear cotton underwear. You aren't out trying to seduce me by pushing your private parts in my face for a quickie. And you don't need attention like the others. You are different. I'll make every part of you mine."

Eric cut through the middle of my blouse and then down each arm. I surmised by doing this; he didn't have to struggle to lift my body to remove my clothing.

"Did you have them on a table, too?" I asked, stalling. The longer he took doing what he wanted, I hoped the effects of the drug wore off.

"Not always. My first was on a table like this one. I took my time with her, too. But the others," he shrugged nonchalantly. "I rushed the others. They didn't deserve more of my time. They weren't worthy. Not like you."

Eric removed the strips from my top and dropped them with the rest of my clothing near the foot of the table.

"You're a beautiful specimen," he whispered to himself, but I heard him since he was so close. If my body wasn't numb, I could feel his breath against my chest.

Eric opened the closet again and removed a small black bag and placed it on my naked stomach. He undid the black bow and unrolled the items stored inside. It felt like a scene from *Dexter*. The only thing missing was plastic on the walls or floor.

"Are you finished?" Thomas yelled, banging on the door.

Eric flinched, dropping the scalpel. He bent down to pick up the blade and scowled. "What did I tell you?" He yelled, placing the scalpel on the bag, and stomped towards the door, yanking it open. "I said I'd call you when I was ready."

When the door opened, the knife pressed against Thomas' neck dug into his soft flesh. The caretaker sliced deeply through Thomas' neck, but then the blade got stuck. The caretaker let go and his body dropped where they stood.

Shocked, Eric just stood there. He didn't have time to defend himself when the caretaker lunged at him, his arms outstretched, and his hands found his neck. He curled his fingers around Eric's neck. The men fell to the ground with the caretaker strangling Eric.

I couldn't see much, but I heard them struggling. Someone grunted, followed by gargling sounds. Something clattered across the floor, then scuttling. Fists flew and lots of grunting.

My right toe moved; it felt cold, and I wiggled my toes but it was only the big toe that moved. I smiled, knowing that soon my whole body would awaken.

"Get off me," Eric yelled. "Oof," he moaned.

They continued fighting, and then something heavy crashed into the tiles.

"Christ, who the fuck was that guy?" Eric said, slowly rising like a nightmare near my feet. He gripped the table for balance, stood straight, and wiped blood off his mouth.

He was quiet for a moment, assessing his injuries when he jerked upright. "Thomas!" He bolted out of the room and into the hallway. He screamed as he cradled his dead brother in his arms.

Seconds passed as I listened to Eric crying in the hall-way. Then there was movement near the table.

"Where did he go?" Eric said. He jumped up and ran down the corridor screaming.

Something grabbed my left arm; I flinched, but I barely moved.

"Ma'am, are you okay?" The caretaker whispered. "My name is Warren. The police are on their way. I need to keep him busy until they arrive."

"Thank you, Warren. You saved my life," I said through thick, dead lips.

"We're not done yet," — he patted my arm again, — "until he's down." He felt his split lip, his fingers coming away with blood. Warren grunted and spat behind him. He grabbed the bag of blades from off my chest, removing the scalpel Eric had wanted to use first. "I'll be right back—"

"No! Please don't leave me alone. Please stay with me until the police come."

"Ma'am, I need to get that guy before he gets you. You understand. I'll lock the room and keep the key with me."

"Please—"

"It will be ok," Warren patted my arm again, but nothing about the action was comforting; I was still numb and didn't want to be locked inside a room by myself.

My toes curled as I moved them, this time on both feet. My skin tingled as my body slowly came to life, reminding me of a trip to the dentist when my gums slowly felt normal.

Warren closed the door behind him. The turning of the lock sounded, and that action filled me with dread.

"Be careful," I whispered but doubted he heard.

Chapter Forty-Three

IT FELT like I'd been lying on the cold table for hours, waiting impatiently for my body to move. The feeling in my toes started coming back, then my feet. But I dared not move my left ankle; it was swollen with multi-colored bruises.

My fingers moved and then my wrists but everything else still felt heavy and cool. The silent room echoed in my ears as I tried listening for signs of life beyond the locked door. There was none.

I hoped Warren got to Eric first.

When something like a siren caught my attention I tried sitting up. My chest ached but my body was still a dead weight.

I flinched when gunshots rang followed by people screaming and running around. The scene sounded like an action movie and I hoped the good guys were winning.

I cried tears of joy when I heard multiple footsteps down the corridor.

"I'm here," I cried out, but it was barely above a whisper. I coughed and cleared my throat.

Someone banged on the door. "Ophelia?" the person spoke on the other side.

"Here," I yelled. "I'm here."

Something hard connected with the door and the lock went flying across the room. The door flew open with a loud bang. Three police officers stood on the other side with a modern battering ram.

The first officer smiled when he saw me, then his face dropped when his eyes roamed over my half-naked body.

The officer handed the battering ram to the guy behind him and hurried inside the room, covering my body with the sheet at my feet.

"You're safe," he said with a twinkle in his eyes. "My name is Reese, and we're here to get you out." He removed his helmet and combed his messy hair. "Where's Piet?" He shouted at the men still standing in the doorjamb.

"On his way," said the other officer now holding the battering ram.

"Can you sit up?" Reese said, reaching for my covered arms and holding on.

"No, he injected me with something and my body is numb." I swallowed hard. It felt like there was cotton wool in my mouth. "I can only move my toes and fingers."

Reese nodded in understanding but I caught hesitation. "We'll wait for the paramedics."

Relief washed over me and I smiled at Reese but he watched the open doorway.

"Where is she? Get out of my way." I knew that was Piet from his heavy Afrikaans accent. "Move!" He pushed the officer out of the way.

Reese stepped to one side, allowing Piet access.

"O, are you okay? What's wrong? Why is she covered?" The lines between his brows deepened and his face was red from running.

"Detective, he drugged her. The paramedics are on their way."

"What drugs? Never mind," Piet said, waving Reese farther away. He reached for my right hand and squeezed. "Jewel is safe and is waiting for you at the hospital."

"Thank you—" I couldn't finish my sentence when I sobbed. Those uncontrollable tears streamed down my face and my chest squeezed.

"Let's get you out of this place. The sooner you're on the ambulance the sooner you'll see Jewel." Piet wrapped me in the sheet and picked me up like I weighed nothing. Reese followed us as we moved through the door and down the corridor.

Noise erupted throughout the house as men wearing black checked each room. While men wearing white protective gear had already started processing parts of the large house for evidence. The smell of gunfire assaulted my nose, but the scent of disinfectant used by the pathologists became overbearing.

With all the commotion, we almost collided with the paramedics. They apologized for almost knocking Piet over and placed the stretcher on the ground. Piet carefully placed me on top of it, ensuring the sheet revealed nothing, and moaned at the paramedics to be careful. They secured me in place and raised the stretcher to wheel me out.

I reached for Piet's hand and didn't want to let go. "Stay with me." I didn't want to be alone with strangers and knew Piet would protect me.

"You know what to do," Piet said to Reese then turned

to me with a smile. "Of course, I'll stay with you." He jerked his chin at the door. "Let's go."

Chapter Forty-Four

ONCE I WAS in the ambulance, two paramedics sat in front while one sat with me. He inserted an IV and checked my vitals. Piet sat near my head, watching the paramedic do his job.

When the paramedic lifted the sheet, exposing my bra, Piet pointed and told him to cover me.

"You're such a good guy," I said, patting his outstretched hand.

"You've been through enough. The last thing you need is some pervert staring at your bra," Piet said, scowling at the paramedic.

I smiled, relieved Piet was on my side. "I assume you guys killed him?"

Piet nodded. "Yep. He first tried to talk his way out, saying it wasn't him, but when he reached for something in his pocket, we fired. He dropped like a sack of farmer's potatoes. We handcuffed his corpse to the gurney."

"What was he reaching for?" I asked, my interest piqued. "What was in his pocket?"

"A scalpel."

I raised my head so I could see Piet. "Was he wearing an overall?"

"Blue ones."

My heart thundered in my chest. They got the wrong guy. "Piet, that's not Eric. He was the caretaker, and he saved me."

Everything happened slowly. The little window near the driver's seat opened. Piet turned to look. The gun fired. Blood splashed across my face. The paramedic crashed into my stomach. I cried out in pain from the impact. Piet turned and fired back. The ambulance swerved. Everything was up in the air then we crashed.

When I awoke, I was on my side lying on top of Piet. He had wrapped his arms around me in a bear hug, shielding me. No one else was awake when the ambulance stopped.

I poked Piet in his side, and he smiled, slowly opening his eyes.

"Are you okay?" I asked, climbing off him.

"My head," he said, rubbing the back of it. "But I'll be ok. How are you?"

"Just bruised, but I'll live." I glanced at my foot, grateful it was already in a type of moon-boot, and the drugs the paramedic had given me were working. "Let's get out of here." I pulled the sheet closer to my half-naked body.

Piet got up first and opened the ambulance doors. He came back inside and picked up his pistol. "Stay here. I need to check first."

"No problem. If you need anything, I'll be right here," I said, pointing at the floor.

Piet chuckled lightheartedly, and then his face fell. He

darted out of the ambulance, walked around the vehicle and opened the driver's side door.

"Freeze!" someone yelled. "Piet, he's running away."

Someone else started shouting, followed by footsteps. Gunshots rang and then silence.

I sat upright. My limbs were finally back to life, but I still couldn't apply pressure on my ankle.

"Piet?" I called, scooting closer to the open doors, keeping the sheet close to my body. "Piet," I yelled and stood on my good foot. I clung to the open door and peered around it. In the distance stood about twenty police officers surrounding a body on the ground, aiming their weapons at him.

Piet glanced up as if sensing my stare and approached, placing his gun back in its holster.

"We have him," he said with the widest smile I'd ever seen.

"I need to see him, Piet. I need to make sure it's him."

"It's him, O. I promise you." Piet closed the distance, the smile on his face splitting his face in two. "I remember his face from when you asked me to check him out, but he was clean. We have him now."

"I don't care. I have to see his body. Please."

Piet conceded and pointed at his back, and crouched. I climbed onto his back so he could give me a piggyback ride. He walked slowly towards the crowd and they quickly dispersed when he yelled at them to make space.

I climbed off Piet's back but held onto his shoulder as I took in the scene. The man who had wreaked havoc these last few weeks was on the ground; blood pulsed out of his neck and chest but there were no signs of life. He had kept the police force on their toes and destroyed so many lives in his wake; he and his brother.

I groaned, remembering Thomas. Now I had to find another employee. But I didn't want to think about that now.

Finally, it was over.

Chapter Forty-Five

BEING PUSHED in a wheelchair out of the hospital was the best feeling ever. I was there for a week and was relieved I could go home. I had the wind at my face, the stale air of hospital food wafting in the background, and Thys's car waiting to take me home.

Jewel bounced up and down. Will stood beside her with a smile and his wife stayed in the car.

"I promise not to bite," I said so only Will could hear.

"I know, but this is about you. We're glad you're okay and going home."

"Thanks," I said, squeezing his shoulder.

The nurse locked the wheelchair in place, and I stood up with my crutches. I had broken five bones in my ankle and two operations later, I could leave. They practically begged me to go, offering free drugs, just to get me out. I kept pointing out various stains on the floors, on the sheets, and in the bathroom with ways to clean them accurately.

"Ready?" Thys asked, holding the car door open for me.

Luckily the bullet had only grazed his hip; ten stitches later he was as good as new.

"Yes, and more than ready for a large glass of wine and a large pizza."

"Yay," Jewel said, followed by a squeal. "Pizza is my favorite."

Will hugged me and Jewel at the same time. "Look after your mom," he said with a wink. "Or she'll beat your ass with her new crutches."

"Bye, Dad," Jewel sang as she climbed into the back seat of Thys's car.

"Chat tomorrow," I said to Will. I handed my crutches to Thys. "Thanks," I said, giving Thys a kiss on the cheek, but he was too quick and turned his face, kissing me on the lips. I smiled as he kissed me; it was one of those kisses filled with purpose and meaning, and I savored the moment.

While I was in the hospital, Thys had visited me twice a day during visiting hours. He smuggled in unhealthy snacks and reprimanded me when I ate them. He made me laugh, and it felt wonderful being around him.

Thys was content going slowly. We were still in the early stages of anything remotely resembling a relationship. Rushing into any kind of relationship would only spell disaster, especially after recent events.

———

ONCE BACK HOME, I propped my foot on the ottoman and leaned back on the couch. My broken ankle would take six to eight weeks to heal and months of physical therapy to get it back into perfect walking shape.

"Nice couch," I said when Jewel entered the lounge. "It's very comfy." I rubbed the soft leather material.

"Thys chose it," she said, wiggling her eyebrows. "How are things going between you two?"

Thys's car roared to life and backed out of the driveway. He had his own remote control for the security gate and closed it behind him. Not that he had a key to the house already, but it made life easier if he had his own remote to enter my yard.

"It's going perfectly slowly. Just the way I like it." I grinned.

"Good, I'm glad you decided on him. He's gorgeous, has his own business, and will keep you in shape. Nobody wants a chubby girlfriend."

"Hey!" — I threw a scatter cushion at her, — "Don't be rude." I laughed when the cushion smacked her in the face.

"Ouch," she said, nursing her nose. "That hurt." She gently threw the cushion back, and it bounced on the seat beside me. "Here's your wine, my lady." She handed me a large glass of red wine; Merlot, my favorite.

"Why thank you, servant. Have you ordered pizza yet?"

Jewel wiggled her eyebrows. "Naturally, only the best for my mother."

When hooting sounded behind us, Jewel opened the curtain to see who was making such a noise. "It's just Jacob with your Ford. I think he's done with the job."

"It will be good to see him."

Jacob had been a star trooper and worked on his own the entire week. After staying off my ankle for another week, I would use a moon boot to get around. I had scenes to clean. Money to make.

Jewel opened the security gate and unlocked the front door. Jacob had his driver's license, but the car I gave him was too small so for the time being he would use my Ford.

"Evening, ladies," Jacob said, entering the house and

closing the front door. "How is the patient doing?" He asked Jewel.

"Already complaining."

"Hey," I said, throwing another scatter cushion at her.

"You missed," she said, darting down the corridor.

"Hi, Jacob. How was it?"

"Easy," he said, sitting on the new leather couch across from me. "These are nice." He rubbed the cushion beneath him.

"I like them too."

"When can you return to work?"

"I'm going to try next week. I should be able to walk then."

"Just don't overexert yourself. Come back when you're ready. Besides, the new guy will start tomorrow, so we don't need you now."

"Gee, thanks. I feel loved."

"You know what I mean."

"I'm just teasing." I adjusted my foot on the ottoman, but the pain was slowly returning. I picked up the pain pills, popped one out of the foil and swallowed it with water. "How was the interview with him?"

"Fine, he heard about Thomas. Apparently, many people had either worked with him or had spoken to him. He attended workshops and conferences on crime scene cleaning and on various cleaning materials. Others speculated he was there looking for lonely women he and his brother could toy with."

I cringed, grateful I didn't go on any dates with these men. "I'm just glad it's all over."

"Me too." Jacob stood again and handed me the car keys. "My family is on their way. I need to fetch them from the bus stop soon."

"That's wonderful news," I said, smiling. "I'll see you tomorrow when you fetch the car again."

"Bye Miss Ophelia."

"Bye Jacob."

As Jacob left on his bicycle, the pizza delivery guy arrived, and Jewel went out to pay. We sat at the table ate our pizza and enjoyed the moments together. I was grateful to still be around. Jewel was safe, and everybody was healthy.

And next week Piet would fetch me so that I could attend his retirement party and give me that drink he promised me.

More from N Gray Writing as Natalie Michaels

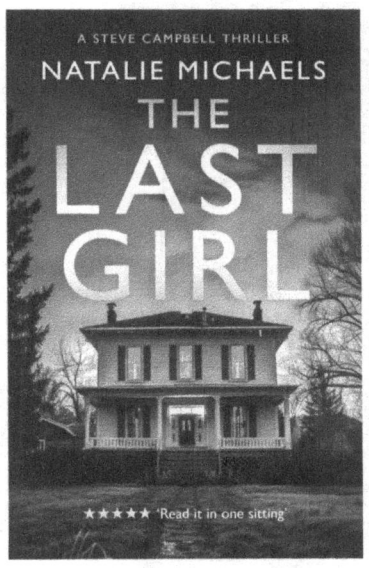

When innocence is stolen, Detective Steve Campbell will stop at nothing for justice in Natalie Michaels' unforgettable thriller, The Last Girl.

Get your copy:

vinci-books.com/campbell1

Turn the page for a free preview

Preview of the Last Girl

1987
  The Cabin
  Jacob

The quiet evening pierced my ears. Carefully, I climbed out of the water and onto the wooden deck without making a sound. I exhaled silently as I monitored the couple fast asleep in the boat. Tiptoeing on the wooden deck, I was careful not to stand on a creaking plank and when I reached the door, Katie stirred in the boat, mumbling someone's name. I opened the door, testing to ensure it didn't moan the wider I opened it, and slipped out.

I traversed the dark path to the house and entered. Leaving the lights off, I navigated my way around the living room, kitchen, until finally upstairs. I entered the main bedroom and found his suitcase again. Flipping through his wallet, I found what I was looking for and headed back down to the kitchen. Their food remained on the counter, waiting for them to enjoy, and I opened the pantry door.

Once done, I slipped out the front door and found a place hidden in shadows where I could see most of the house and waited. I heard cars driving on the ID-75 entering and exiting Ketchum and was grateful they were a distance away and wouldn't see me or my vehicle from the road.

It was ten at night by the time Katie and her friend staggered up the path, switching on lights as they entered the house and headed for the kitchen. Katie warmed their dinner while her friend sat at the table, waiting for her to serve him.

The itch at the back of my neck started up again, but I didn't scratch. I just rubbed the offending area and waited.

Katie dished food onto their plates and sat beside him. My body heated as I watched him eat. All was fine for a few seconds and then... he grabbed his throat. His eyes widened in horror. Red blotches formed on his face and neck. His face started swelling, along with one side of his neck. He pushed away from the table, stood up, then doubled over as if trying to expel whatever was lodged in his throat.

Katie was there to slap him on his back, but nothing helped.

Nothing would help him.

The man pointed to the stairs and then to his neck. Katie nodded and frantically ran upstairs.

Moments later, she returned, shaking her head. "There's nothing there," she cried.

Shock flashed in his eyes. He collapsed onto his knees, then fell on his chest and face, unmoving.

Katie dashed around, looking for something, but there was nothing that could help him. She fell to her knees and moved him onto his back so she could proceed with CPR, but his throat had already closed, shutting off all his air supply.

From where I stood, his face and neck had swollen to the point where his cheeks were red, round and puffy, and his eyes had bulged. While his fat lips had started turning purple.

After about ten minutes, Katie sat back on her haunches, crying into her hands.

I dropped the epinephrine injection on the ground and crushed it with my boot heel. Pushing through the branches, I approached the cabin with purpose and entered through the front door.

Katie flinched when she saw me and stood up. "Jacob, what are you doing here?" she asked, glancing nervously at me and then at her friend on the floor.

"I thought you might need some help," I said mysteriously and crossed the threshold. My clothing was still damp, and I left wet marks everywhere I stepped.

Katie backed up, glancing at me and the body. "We need to call for help," she stammered, "could you—"

"No," I yelled, shutting her up. "No more, Katie," I snapped. "You've been playing me for years. No more." I pulled the box out of my pocket and placed it gently on the counter. "I've had this for a while, waiting for the right moment to give it to you. To ask for your hand in marriage. Ever since that day in the barn, I've loved you more than anything else. I would've given you the world, anything, and everything you ever wanted. But," I paused for effect and stared into her sad, blue eyes, "you've made it perfectly clear where I stand with you."

2001

The Second Week in December
Michelle

Jessica combed her long blond hair and tied it in a low ponytail. She fixed her black top; the one I had bought her for her birthday with the famous Rolling Stones tongue. Then she fastened her belt and pulled on her coat. Grabbing her makeup bag, she applied eyeshadow, mascara that made her green eyes brighter, and lipstick sparingly, transforming her youthful face into a more mature look.

We had become best friends since first grade in the Ernest Hemingway School in Ketchum. Since then, we did nothing without the other. Once a month, we visited Mike, our good friend, and went to O'Brian's Pub for a few beers and a couple of games.

"How do I look?" she asked, twirling.

"Like you're twenty-two," I said, grinning. I pulled on my coat and huddled into it. "How about me?"

"Perfect," she said.

I wiped some makeup out of the corner of my eye and smiled. My eyes had thick eyeliner, highlighting my big brown eyes, and I tied my black hair in a low ponytail. I had a fair complexion and with my hair being naturally black; I looked like a porcelain doll. But I was not as beautiful as Jessica.

"Are you two wenches finished?" Mike yelled outside the bathroom. "I'm hungry, and there's a game with my name on."

"Yeah, yeah, we're done," I said, opening the door.

Mike stood in the doorjamb, blocking my way. He wore

his signature black outfit; black army boots, black cargo pants, and a long sleeve black vest with a black jacket over. With his brown hair shaved close to his head, he reminded me of someone who should be in the army and not out drinking.

I waved the air in front of my nose. "You smell like weed again."

"I know. You want some?"

"No, thanks."

"Come," Jessica said, pushing past Mike, "there are men who need to buy us drinks."

"You're such a skank," Mike said, chuckling, his smile reaching his light brown eyes. If it wasn't for the gothic clothing he wore, I thought he was handsome.

"You're just jealous you can't get free drinks." She cooed.

"Whatever, now come," Mike said, jogging down the stairs. "Bye mom," he yelled into the lounge. His mom waved and continued watching her fantasy series.

We climbed into Mike's blue van, his Passion Wagon, and drove the short distance to O'Brian's Pub. It was a quaint little drinking hole where a lot of the residents frequented. The place smelled like stale ale. The bar counter was sticky from years of spillage, and the beer flowed all night long.

Mike parked the van in the only available parking spot, which was right at the back underneath the one lamppost that didn't work. We traversed the recently cleared path as snow continued falling around us.

I entered the pub first, and the heat smacked me in the face. Shivering from the sudden change in temperature, I headed for the bar and stood between two men talking about their workday.

"Oh, I'm sorry. Am I bothering you?" I asked, fluttering my eyelashes.

"No, sweetheart," the man on my right said. "But I would love to buy you a drink?"

"A beer will do," I said, smiling sweetly.

"Hey Nancy," said the same man, "get my lady friend here a beer."

"Make that two, please, kind sir," Jessica said behind me.

"Make it two," he said with a wicked grin. "And who might you be?"

"Jessica," she said, holding out her hand for him to shake.

Nancy gave us our beers.

The man stood to retrieve his wallet from his back pocket, paid, and sat down again. Jessica and I stood on either side of him and kissed him on the cheek.

"Thank you," we said together and disappeared into the crowd near the back, where Mike was already playing a game of pool.

We laughed and joked around. We tampered with Mike's cue stick every time he tried to take a shot, sipped from his friends' drinks, and enjoyed our evening.

I loved coming here, as did Jessica. We were together, we always had fun, and we never had to pay for anything.

"I feel like a shot," Jessica said, swaying slightly.

"You've had enough," I said, slipping my arm through hers. "How about we ask Nancy for something to eat and two glasses of water?"

"Nah, I want a shot." Jessica unhooked her arm from mine and made a beeline toward the bar. She bumped into a man wearing a blue jacket sitting at the bar and started talking to him. She laughed at whatever he said and sat beside him. They seemed to enjoy each other's company and now and then, Jessica would touch his arm or laugh at whatever he said. Then she thumbed over her shoulder at me. But the man didn't turn around.

Mike cut in front of me, blocking my view. "Move," I moaned and pushed past him. When I could see Jessica again, she downed a shot with the man and then he stood up from his stool. He pointed at the door, and Jessica nodded.

"What are you doing?" I mumbled to myself.

"Where are you going?" Mike asked.

"To stop Jessica from making a big mistake."

"She's a big girl. She can take care of herself."

"She's only nineteen, Mike," I grumbled. "We need to look out for each other."

Mike raised his hands in mock surrender. "Fine, but if you aren't here when I'm ready to go, I'll leave your ass here, too."

I rolled my eyes and headed for the door. Jessica and the man had already left by the time I pulled on my coat. I opened the door, and the cold air stole my breath as I braved the chilly night.

A car's engine rumbled to life in the distance, and I turned to look, but couldn't see much. A light came on and I squinted.

"Jessica?" I yelled and headed for the car. "Jessica?" I yelled again, waving my arms so she could see me.

A car door slammed, and a figure headed my way. "Michelle," Jessica said, closing the gap. "I'm going home with my new friend." She wiggled her eyebrows. "I'll see you at Mike's tomorrow," she slurred, hugging me. When she let me go, her now dull green eyes glazed over as she smiled.

"Are you sure you're in condition to go home with anyone?" I asked.

"Relax, I'm fine. Besides, everyone knows him," she said, turning around.

"Who is he?" I asked. There were moments like now when I hated going out with Jessica. She had gone home with guys once or twice before, but I had always met them beforehand. I didn't know who this guy was, and it left me worried.

"It's fine, he's fine, I'm fine," she mumbled. "I'll see you in the morning." She waved over her shoulder as she walked to his car.

"Who is he?" I yelled, but she didn't hear me.

Once Jessica climbed into his car, he turned around, blinding me with his headlights. Once I could see again, all I saw were his taillights in the distance.

I didn't like her going off with some stranger she had only just met and even though he was someone everybody knew, apparently; I didn't know who he was.

Something didn't sit right with me, but I shook off the bad feeling. She was a young adult and could handle herself.

When I went back inside the pub, I had sobered up and asked Mike if we could leave. He handed me the keys and asked me to drive.

Once back at his place, I settled into the bed beside him, and he started snoring; I laid awake with worry.

***

The next morning, when Jessica didn't come home, I asked Mike to take me to the police station. I waited to speak with an officer, filled out forms, and explained what had happened.

When Monday came and went and Jessica still hadn't come home, and I hadn't heard from the detective, I went back to the police station. They reassured me they were investigating and would give me feedback by Wednesday.

Wednesday passed, and the detective called me on Thursday to let me know they had no leads or witnesses. He also informed me that there were many people at O'Brian's Pub and Nancy didn't remember Jessica or me being there, therefore nobody knew who the man was she had gone home with.

When Friday arrived and I still had heard nothing, I asked Mike to go with me to the pub, but because Christmas was next Tuesday, he was taking his mother to visit his aunt in Sun Valley.

I went alone to the pub, but it was empty, with only a few patrons; none of them remembered me and I couldn't recall them either. I came home early and vowed to go the next weekend and the next until I found out who Jessica's kidnapper was.

If he was local, he had to return.

Get your copy:
vinci-books.com/campbell1

Notes from the author

I started writing Lady Killer in 2021, then I had to put it one side to write the paranormal romance books I had to get out due to prior commitments.

Then 2022 came along and I was burnt out so I took it easy during the year and took my time finishing Lady Killer.

Ophelia is a strong woman who still has her own weaknesses when times were tough. Whose flight-or-fight responses are perfect, I know mine aren't… perhaps I should join a self-defense class or two.

And the spots where the bodies were dumped were based on hiking trails I'd hiked during 2022.

Here in the Western Cape there's always something to do if you have the energy, and the views really are breath-taking. I love my beach walks, shorter hikes, and wine tasting.

And unfortunately, the crime is bad but the police force do their best to keep us safe. Should you ever visit our lovely country, just be vigilant and you should be fine.

That's it from me. Stay safe, keep reading, and come say *hi* on my social media pages or email me.